SMOKE AGAINST THE SKY

It was Cheyenne country, and the smoke signals against the sky spelled death to the peace between red and white men for which Captain David Moncure had been hoping. Fort Starke was the logical place to go for help, but the commanding officer there was a man who knew just enough about Moncure's past to think him a traitor, and it was impossible for the captain to reveal the truth about his wartime experiences, or to reveal that his brother, and the woman Moncure loved, had been captured by the Indians. If he could overcome the obstacles posed by white hostility, Moncure intended to bring about the return of all captives— including the two people most important in his life . . .

SMOKE AGAINST THE SKY

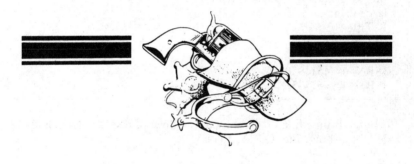

Lynn Westland

ATLANTIC LARGE PRINT
Chivers Press, Bath, England.
Curley Publishing, Inc.,
South Yarmouth, Mass., USA.

Library of Congress Cataloging in Publication Data

Westland, Lynn, 1899–
    Smoke against the sky / Lynn Westland.
        p.   cm.—(Atlantic large print)
    ISBN 1–55504–902–8 (lg. print)
    1. Large type books.   I. Title.
[PS3519.O712S56 1989]
813'.54—dc19   89–30258
                                                                                    CIP

British Library Cataloguing in Publication Data

Westland, Lynn, *1899–*
    Smoke against the sky.—(Atlantic
    large print)
    I. Title
    813'.52 [F]

    ISBN 0–7451–9501–6
    ISBN 0–7451–9513–X Pbk

This Large Print edition is published by Chivers Press, England, and
Curley Publishing, Inc, U.S.A. 1989

Published by arrangement with Donald MacCampbell, Inc

U.K. Hardback ISBN 0 7451 9501 6
U.K. Softback ISBN 0 7451 9513 X
U.S.A. Softback ISBN 1 55504 902 8

SMOKE AGAINST THE SKY

CHAPTER ONE

Once more, and for the third time that day, there was smoke against the sky, puffing up mockingly in places distant from where Captain David Moncure rode; smoke signals placed as though to irritate and tantalize, propounding a riddle: How could there be peace between red man and white, while talk of war was so literally in the air?

He had been two days on the trail on this particular scout, out from Fort Lansing where it squatted on a tributary of the Paradise. That a part at least of the answer he sought lay in the smoke he had no doubt, and he rode with increasing grimness as he suspected what it must inevitably prove.

Leanly erect in the saddle, a reddish stubble of beard coating a long jaw, blending to darker sideburns under startlingly blue eyes, Moncure looked what he was, a soldier by profession and inclination. A few sprinkles of gray at the temples lent an air of distinction.

He rode alone, which was nothing new, any more than was the risk he was taking. Danger had ruled the land for the past decade, nor had surrender and the faint haze of peace driven it to cover.

Though he had been bending south since dawn, he was still in Cheyenne country. And

1

despite a multitude of rumors concerning a new era of good will between white men and red, even dispatches from headquarters about the proposed return of all white captives held across the long span of the years, still it *was* Cheyenne country; a land of bending horizons and endless plains, of sudden mountains slashing the sky, of driving storms and smiling suns, and of secret arrows tipped with death.

This was the afternoon of his second day, and by rights he should be heading back. The tentative limit of his quest had been passed hours ago, and still he'd kept on south, feeling a pull, as though somehow the solution might lie over the next rise. Now, by his best calculations, he was considerably closer to Fort Starke than to Lansing.

Thrice the day before he'd also caught glimpses of smoke on the horizon, staining the sky above sprawls of rimrocks. Such signals were tantalizing. They were as ancient as the Indians, known almost ever since the discovery of how to rub two sticks together and produce fire. Smoke talk was a universal language, which could be seen far on a clear day; read and relayed, the message could outstrip the fastest horse. Even the talking wire of the white man, spreading like the strands of a spider's web, could barely outrun it.

Moncure's difficulty was that he was never

able to catch more than a glimpse or so before it was gone. What he had been able to read was inconclusive, but he had the haunted sense that the smoke talk dealt somehow with himself.

It was past time to be turning back, by any reasonable standard of safety; also, he lacked supplies. He still had a small, flint-like chunk of pemmican, which could stave off hunger and furnish energy better than most rations devised by the white man. The combination of sun-dried buffalo meat and wild berries was even tasty, though as with many things Indian, a taste had to be developed.

Nowhere had he found that which was the principal object of his search: a cache of arms. Colonel Neilson had concurred in his opinion that modern rifles were being supplied to the red men, despite all the pipes of peace and watchfulness of the garrison at Fort Lansing. There was an ironic optimism in the notion that a few score men in blue could police a territory whose magnitude dwellers along the eastern shore could barely imagine. And if, as they suspected, there was treachery from white men in high places, the problem became staggeringly more difficult.

There had been new quality to the whispering campaign in these last weeks, a specious sort of reasonableness which caused Moncure's suspicions to raise like the hackles on a wolf. There was the suggestion that the prospects of peace might be enhanced by a demonstration of trust and good will, by furnishing the Indians the modern rifles they desired; rifles for the hunting of buffalo and bear, to insure an adequate food supply. Guns thus given, it was implied, would not be used against the white man.

Moncure dismissed such reasoning for what it was worth. The truth was that Cheyenne or Sioux, Blackfoot or Crow, were more deadly at slaying buffalo with bows and arrows than was the white man with his long rifle, shot for shot. Crowding his cayuse close alongside the lumbering giants, the Indian lacked food only when the buffalo became a ghost herd on the purple plain.

It was not that he had really expected to stumble upon a cache, or even any sure sign; Moncure was taking this ride to test the wind, somewhat after the manner of the wolf, or of wild geese in flight. However empty the horizon, the wolf could scent game across far reaches, and the gray goose received the warning of storm long before it came howling out of the arctic wastes.

Moncure laid no claim to possessing such sure instincts, but like his forerunner of an earlier generation, the Mountain Man, he could read sign and smell trouble. What the Indians called medicine, white men termed a hunch. It was not the name which counted; a winter ermine was no less deadly when transformed by summer to a hue of soft brown.

Sound broke sharply on the drowsing afternoon—the whang of a smooth-bore rifle, akin to the cough of a startled grizzly. Its echo seemed to set atremble the leaves of a clump of aspen, huddled together at the rim of a coulee which gashed the plain.

The gunshot had come from beyond the coulee, where the land lay twisted and broken. It was followed by two other bursts, one the sharper sound of a Colt, the other akin to the first, though different. Guns, like men or cattle or beasts of the field, spoke with individual voices. Some ears were trained to distinguish between nuances of sound, while others detected no differences.

Having heard many guns in his time, Moncure had no trouble interpreting these shots. First a rifle had spoken; then its intended victim had dragged at his own six-gun, getting off a shot in turn. Only one, before a second rifle took up the chant, summarily ending the dialogue.

There was silence now, a hush strongly suggesting that the drama was played out and done with, as, most likely, was its victim. Moncure hesitated briefly, weighing his course, then put his horse to a run toward the spot where the sounds had erupted. He might be tempting fate, and to no purpose. But Indians seldom had six-guns, and white men

5

went to the aid of their fellows.

Equally important in his thinking was the certainty that this was an attack, evidence of the treachery which he was out to find. Talk of peace, like rising smoke, could hide more than it revealed.

One cry arose, a gobbling shout; then there was silence again. It required all his resolution to keep going, for the sound was Indian, some sort of order, and warriors might come sweeping at him at any instant. None did, as he reached a crest and slowed, his puzzlement matching his alarm. There had been no other sound, no shouts of triumph, no shrilling war whoops.

The bewildering part was that there was no sign of the attackers. Every indication, including that single shouted order, was that they had been Indians. It was more than odd that they would suddenly vanish at his approach, not even lingering to take the scalp of their victim.

Almost certainly they had seen or heard him as he came, and had withdrawn. Possibly they had feared that he was one of a much larger force, though the explanation did not satisfy him. Such action ran counter to all rules and customs.

It would not take long to get out of sight in such broken country. Indians were as adept at disappearing acts as a covey of young prairie chickens.

But by now they would realize that they had been mistaken, that he was alone, riding toward the wagon. Moncure had the sensation of eyes boring into his back, the crawling expectation of arrow or bullet. Still, it was as safe to go ahead as to crouch and shiver, since he had already been seen.

Expecting the attack to resume, he rode warily, but nothing happened. Dismounting, he was surprised to find the man still alive. The bullet had passed through his body, further proof that it had been fired at close range. The shoulder wound was bleeding.

Moncure had seen many wounds. This he judged to be a borderline case, where the lead had missed lungs and heart alike. Had either of them been punctured, the man would be dead, or the bleeding greatly increased. Thus, if afforded proper care, the victim might have a chance of survival.

A growth of tufted light beard lent a curiously jaunty look to the face, even in strained repose. The wounded man's six-shooter lay beside his hand in the bottom of the wagon box, and a well-filled cartridge belt was about his waist. There was no rifle.

The injured man carried a blue bandana. Torn in two, it served as pads for the wound. His shirt, pulled off and wrapped around, then tied by the sleeves, held the bandages in place. The bleeding was pretty well stanched.

Still anticipating a bullet or sudden rush,

7

Moncure worked tensely. The silence was broken as a cricket set up its chirping from deep in the grass. By a long stretch of the imagination, it might be called the grass beside the road. There was a wheel trace there where occasional wagons had passed, bringing supplies up from Fort Starke to Lansing.

The regular route lay a quarter of a mile to the west, but a patch of ground, swampy after rain, caused some drivers to swing off, circling, then cutting back.

Few vehicles had used the road of late. Despite the talk and rumors of amity, the tenuous peace had been fractured by attacks on supply wagons, only one of which had succeeded in reaching Fort Lansing in the last month. A shortage of many items was beginning to be acute.

There was no indication that this wagon had been headed for Fort Lansing, or that it had carried any supplies. Apparently he'd been heading south by east, toward Starke, coming from the west. Stagecoaches and some other travel followed that road, which had been less subject to attack.

The unhurt horse had stopped trembling, growing accustomed to the smell of its companion's blood. Moncure got the harness off the dead animal, surprised that there were no breaks in it. He led the other horse to the side, straightening it again in the traces. Still there was no interruption, no sign of the original attackers. The mystery was hard to explain, but fortunate if it lasted.

Grimly, Moncure decided upon a plan of action, one hardly to his liking. By rights he should return to Lansing, since he was already overdue. At Lansing was Karl Hochhalter, the bristly-bearded physician who had studied at Vienna, then turned to save a few poor devils along a far frontier.

On the other hand, he was a dozen miles beyond the halfway point between Forts Lansing and Starke, a difference of more than a score of miles in favor of Starke. Since Starke had its own regimental physician, he owed it to the injured man to get him to the nearest help in the shortest possible time.

One horse could not pull the wagon, which was designed for a team. He led his own pony alongside, on the opposite side of the wagon tongue, adjusting the harness without removing the saddle. The feel of the saddle would be a powerful reassurance, since the cayuse was accustomed to it.

The two animals regarded each other somewhat askance, but both were tired from long hours at a steady pace, so there was no open hostility. His own pony resisted again when he removed its bridle and substituted that of the dead animal; it mouthed the strange bit restively.

He gathered sagebrush, working with

increasing confidence as a lark took up its song, an indication that no skulkers were about. There was a blanket in the wagon box, as well as his own, tied to the back of his saddle. He spread these over the mattress of sage, stretching the wounded man as comfortably as possible. Then, taking up the reins, talking soothingly to the horses, he climbed to the wagon seat. There was blood in the bottom of the box, but none where his predecessor had sat.

For a few minutes it was touch and go whether or not his saddle horse would work in traces and tandem, pulling a wagon. But the saddle was reassuring, as was Moncure's untroubled voice. The other horse led out strongly, anxious to get away from so unpleasant a place. Presently they were snaking the light wagon along at a steady trot.

Nothing amiss was to be seen, but he drove with rifle ready to his grasp, his gaze as restless as a hawk's. It was a relief to hear the faint boom of the sunset gun at Fort Starke. There was enough light remaining for him to espy the outlines of the stockade as he approached, still not quite believing his luck.

The gate had been closed for the night, but at his hail an officer appeared, venturing out as the sentry stood with rifle at the ready. He had a look over the edge of the wagon box, then peered more closely up at Moncure and saluted smartly. Presently the doctor was in charge, and Moncure was being led away to report to the commandant.

He went with a slight shrug. This was according to custom and regulation, and there was nothing to do but acquiesce. It was one of the hazards of duty. He did not look forward to the meeting.

Major Peter O'Day commanded at Starke, and there was a coolness between the commandants at Starke and Lansing. Most of it was due to jealous resentment on O'Day's part. Starke, if anything, was more important than Lansing, yet he held only the rank of major, while Neilson, at Lansing, was a full colonel. It made no difference that Neilson, during the war not too lately ended, had been breveted a brigadier a full year before Lee's surrender.

Also, it irked O'Day that Neilson had been trained at The Point, whereas his own knowledge of soldiering had been gleaned while rising from the ranks. It had undoubtedly reached his ears that Captain Moncure, Neilson's new second in command, had also been a West Pointer.

The smell of food, the roast ribs of buffalo and the even more tantalizing aroma of coffee, tickled Moncure's nostrils as he crossed the parade ground. Sharply conscious of his hunger, he shrugged the thought aside, then paused as someone else all but collided with him as the door was opened from within.

Another tantalizing, almost forgotten fragrance was wafted on the air, the richness of a gentlewoman's perfume. How long had it been since he'd known such a scent? Too long, by any standards.

She stopped with a surprised exclamation, looking at him, and Moncure was aware of a piquant face, framed by a bonnet-like hat, of brown eyes beneath brown curls, of a saucily uptilted nose. She stood to one side as Moncure bowed, and the flustered lieutenant rigidly saluted the man looming behind her, introducing Moncure as briefly as possible.

A kerosene lamp burned on the desk, giving off a stench from an imperfectly trimmed and burning wick. O'Day stared, astonishment further reddening a ruddy pair of cheeks above a sweeping brush of mustache.

'Moncure? Now what the devil's this? You're Dunstan—and a traitor to boot!'

CHAPTER TWO

Having been aware that Peter O'Day was commandant at Fort Starke, Moncure was not surprised at the greeting. Ordinarily, on his way up from Arizona to Lansing, he would have spent a night at Starke, but he'd bypassed it with deliberate intent. This time,

12

with a man's life at stake, that had been impossible.

That he understood O'Day's mistrust scarcely made the situation any better. O'Day knew that David Dunstan had been a lieutenant in the Army of the United States, serving with distinction against the Indians in the West until late in '62. Then, transferred East, he had resigned his commission, apparently unwilling to serve against the Confederacy.

Not many men knew that part of his history, though some, like O'Day, believed that they knew. It was impossible to explain, now as it had been then, that he had obeyed a request from higher authority, vanishing below the Mason-Dixon line to continue a mission at which he had already been working for more than a year.

His task had been no ordinary sort of espionage. He had been as eager as his superiors to track down and destroy a ring of traitors, men no more loyal to the South than to the North, whose activities had been dedicated solely to personal profit; vultures preying on victims of the struggle and possessed of the carrion instincts of such creatures.

His first encounter with the ring had revealed certain men conniving with Indians otherwise inclined to be friendly, setting them upon a course of pillage and murder against helpless settlers, or wives and children of men off to war on one side or the other. For such conduct there was no military or patriotic justification, from it no result save confusion and grief, but to the perpetrators, frequently it brought rich plunder.

Encouraged by initial successes, the ring had grown, enlarging their operations. In time, both sides had become equally anxious to have them ferreted out and destroyed, and it had fallen to Moncure to carry out that secret vendetta during the last two years of the war.

In the West, because it had seemed helpful, he had been known as Lieutenant David Dunstan. Later, he'd used not his middle but his last name, deliberately adding to the confusion, by war's end winning the right to the commission of full colonel. Most of the ring had been wiped out, but that was still a secret, since at least some of that infamous company were still uncaught.

Peter O'Day had been briefly involved, and he was ever a man to jump to conclusions. Moncure saluted even as he shrugged.

'Your accusation, Major O'Day, borders on the intemperate. My commanding officer, as well as others, have seen fit to give me a position of trust.'

'The more fools they,' O'Day stormed. 'I wouldn't have a turncoat rebel serving under me, regardless of policy in Washington.'

14

Becoming aware of the sharp interest not merely of the lady, but also of the lieutenant, he controlled himself with an effort, then grudgingly acknowledged the courtesy due to the uniform.

'My dear, this is Captain Moncure—or so it appears—from Fort Lansing. Captain, Miss Serena Sullivan, niece of your commanding officer at Lansing.'

Eyes bright, lips slightly parted and head tilted to one side, Serena Sullivan had been watching with quickening interest. Moncure read something akin to approval in her glance as he made his reply; clearly, as the niece of a soldier, she had learned to form her own judgments. She smiled slightly, then, appearing not to notice how O'Day's face purpled, extended her hand.

'From Fort Lansing, Captain Moncure? I am on my way there—for a surprise visit, you might say.'

Accepting her handshake, Moncure caught his breath in surprise. Such news could be good, yet bad at the same time.

'I'm sure it will be a pleasant surprise for Colonel Neilson,' he observed.

O'Day interrupted. He clearly did not like her acceptance of a man he had just denounced, but he could hardly tell his guest so.

'May I ask what brings you here, Captain?' he asked.

15

Moncure explained, while all of them remained standing. Serena Sullivan was clearly loath to go, O'Day somewhat at a loss as to how to deal with the situation. He listened to the story in silence, but with raised eyebrows, as Moncure described what he knew of the attack which had wounded the man with the wagon.

'Indians?' he repeated. 'Isn't that a somewhat far-fetched assumption, Captain? At the present time, the Indians are on their good behaviour, more than usually so if anything, and you know as well as I do that if it had been Indians who had made such an attack, they would certainly have followed it up.'

Logic was on his side, and Moncure knew better than to argue the matter. But he had not foreseen the consequences of such an assumption, which became apparent later in the evening. By then he had enjoyed a good meal, afterward paying a call upon the wounded man, who had regained consciousness after being cared for by the doctor. The latter gave it as his opinion that the man stood a good chance of recovering.

He eyed Moncure gravely, speaking barely above a whisper to express his gratitude.

'I'd have been a goner, with my hair lifted, but for you,' he observed. 'I sure thought they had me.'

'You saw who jumped you?' Moncure

16

asked.

'Indians. Cheyennes, I figure, but I couldn't be sure about that. Maybe a dozen of 'em—they came out of nowhere right sudden. Led by a big chief.'

That confirmed Moncure's original guess, though it increased his bewilderment that they should have withdrawn in such fashion, after seeing that their victim was alone. He was emboldened to request the loan of the injured man's horse and wagon for his return to Fort Lansing the next day. It would be more dangerous than traveling on horseback; still, he'd had a few charmed hours with it during the afternoon, and he could take along some much needed supplies and outrun heavier supply wagons by a couple of days. Major O'Day had informed him that fresh ones had arrived and would also be leaving the next day.

'Sure, you're more'n welcome to borrow my outfit,' the injured man granted permission. 'I won't be needin' 'em for quite a while—and I never would again, but for you.'

Moncure planned to set out on the return trip bright and early. What he had not counted on was Serena Sullivan's request to be allowed to accompany him.

'I'm on my way to visit my uncle and aunt, and I'm afraid that I also took Major O'Day by surprise, arriving as I did,' she confessed,

17

with just a hint of a smile which Moncure found charming. 'I'll probably startle Uncle Myles just as much—but I hope it won't be an unpleasant surprise. You don't mind if I go with you, do you, Captain?'

It was a difficult question to which to reply. Certainly he had no objection to such charming and unexpected company, over the long miles which lay ahead. The prospect held a fairy-tale quality.

On the other hand, there had been a murderous attack on the wagon only today, and aside from such risks, he had a feeling that Fort Lansing, isolated as it was, might soon become more of an outpost than it already was.

There was also O'Day, glowering in the background; he realized that the major's patent dislike for him was an important factor.

Nonetheless, he had to point out the dangers of such a course. Serena listened, then countered as he had expected:

'But you're making the trip back, Captain!'

'That's my job,' he pointed out. 'But should I undertake to escort Colonel Neilson's niece, and then should something happen—'

Major O'Day had been listening with scarcely concealed impatience. He seemed to feel that the wounded man's testimony about Indians having attacked him was a deliberate

18

affront to himself, contrived to place him in an untenable position. He broke in now.

'I'm sure that the risk is slight,' he said. 'If I believed otherwise, I would not give my consent. I'll confess to personal feelings where Captain *Moncure* is concerned, but that is your affair, my dear—and in such a matter I'm sure he's trustworthy. I could send you along with the supply wagons, but a team and light wagon will be much faster and more comfortable. You should feel complimented, sir, that so lovely a lady chooses to grant you her company.'

'I am, Major, indeed I am,' Moncure agreed. 'Since she is to go along, may I request an escort? I believe it would be a sensible precaution.'

He saw by the major's eyes that he was inclined to refuse, principally because it was Moncure who had made the request. Then, glancing again at Serena, mindful of the rank of her uncle, he shrugged and conceded the point.

'Very well. I'll send a couple of outriders along with you. So rare a visitor to our country deserves an escort. I'm only sorry that you can't remain longer among us here at Fort Starke, my dear.'

It *was* pleasant to journey with such a companion on the seat beside him, this time with the blankets folded as padding beneath them. It was abundantly clear that she had not been influenced by O'Day's impulsive charge of treason. Accustomed to the Army and its ways, she clearly trusted the judgment of those who had seen fit to accept Moncure for what he was, and she was doing the same. For that he was humbly grateful.

As the miles lengthened and the sun grew hot, he grew more and more watchful, despite the two horsemen who rode some distance ahead. He drove mechanically. Then, at a low, half-amused, half-mocking laugh, he glanced quickly at his companion, then as swiftly away. Even in that brief look, he was more than ever aware of the entrancing profile of throat and chin, of strength masked by soft contours, of eyes which held a glint of amusement.

'You seem intent upon the skyline, Captain.' Serena's voice was demure, but he suspected that she was laughing at him.

'That's true, Miss Sullivan,' he acknowledged. 'I have been watching it. There's smoke off there.'

'Smoke?' Her attention quickened; then she shaded her eyes against the sun. 'I hadn't noticed. You have good eyes.'

'They have been trained to keep alert, ma'am. That is the first safety measure in this country.'

'Do you mean—Indians, again?' The final word implied she accepted his judgment, as against that of O'Day. There was a catch in her breath, but a sidelong glance revealed her cheeks were no less pink, held no sudden pallor of fear.

'I suspect it must be Indians. Whites seldom indulge in such a practice.'

'Forgive me.' Her voice was demure again. 'Now I know why you looked everywhere but at me. For a while I thought it might be because you were afraid of me.'

This gentle raillery whetted his own mettle, though it was a long time since he had played such games. 'Should not I be, ma'am?'

'I don't think so,' she replied. 'I am not a man-eater, Captain Moncure. Nor am I accustomed to "ma'am" or "Miss Sullivan." You shroud me with an impossible dignity. I'm simply Serena Sullivan to my friends.'

'To be counted among your friends is a high privilege,' he assured her gravely. 'In that case, my name is David.'

'That's much better, I think. Also, I appreciate you giving me a ride under these conditions. Will my uncle be surprised, do you think? I know I should have written, but I found myself homesick for the boom of the evening gun, the flag lonely above a wilderness, a bugle at dawn—and I yielded to impulse.'

'A gracious impulse, to allow us old soldiers a glimpse of beauty. No doubt he will be surprised—also, the colonel will be entranced and dismayed. The young officers will be delighted.'

'The others, but not you, David?' He sensed that she was laughing at him, as he suspected had been more or less the case since the ride had begun at dawn. She had been ready when he'd come for her, fresh as the morning and unafraid, and she had endured the jolting and hardship without a word of complaint. In mid-afternoon she still looked as fresh as she had at sunrise. Which, of course, was only to be expected of the daughter of a captain of artillery, the niece of a colonel of cavalry.

'Serena,' he answered, and his voice was suddenly grave, 'I suspect that you, being a woman, young and beautiful to boot, might like to enliven so wearying a ride as this with a bit of harmless flirtation. For my part, I'd enjoy nothing better—except that, as a soldier, I recognize the smell of powder. With so weathered a relic as myself, you would risk nothing, experience nothing to cause your heart to palpitate even a fraction of a beat faster. With me it would be quite the contrary. I might lose my head—or my heart—very easily.'

She caught her breath at his sudden frankness, then, meeting his eyes, colored and smiled.

'So you *do* have a heart, Captain? I had been led to wonder. For myself, I admit the charge—I indulged in a bit of idle flirtation.

But I can't concede the rest, that the danger might all be on one side. You are neither so old nor so weathered as to be unattractive in the eyes of a woman.'

'You are kind,' he murmured. 'So I'll confess something else. Somewhat more than a year ago, I was engaged to another, and most charming lady.'

'And she jilted you, shaking your faith in all my sex?'

'No. Had it been only that—' His jaw, for an instant, took on the aspect of a sprung steel trap. 'She has been a captive of the Kiowas, and no trace has been found of her since.'

'A captive of the Indians? Oh, I'm sorry.' Serena's hand moved on impulse, resting lightly on his own. It was as quickly withdrawn, but he sensed her genuine sympathy. 'But this is Cheyenne country.'

'Until a few weeks ago, I was stationed in Kiowa territory—and I combed it rather thoroughly.' His eyes were again on the distant puffs of smoke, staining the sky above the line of rimrocks. 'That's why,' he added. 'I don't know what may have happened, in some twenty months' time. Only it was not her fault. I still hope.'

'Of course. I've been hearing talk as I journeyed West, so I understand that there's soon to be a meeting of many tribes, at which time the Indians are to return all their white

23

captives.'

'Your news is later than mine, though such talk has been in the wind. Perhaps it will come off. Personally, I'm not hopeful of the results.'

'Not hopeful? But I know that many people are very much excited at the prospect—'

'That's because hope is slow in dying—and many of them don't know Indians—or how white captives turn Indian,' he said grimly. 'If it does come off, I doubt that it will be a cause for much rejoicing on either side.'

'You are suggesting that my uncle, the colonel, will find me an added responsibility at a time when he's already overtaxed with duties?'

'Your uncle and aunt will be delighted to see you. I was speaking personally. Most people think that this proposed return of captives is a good sign, an indication of peace between red men and white. I wish I could share in such optimism, but I have a feeling that the whole thing is a trick, a cover-up for greater mischief. Out of it could perhaps come war on a wider scale than the border has ever known. So I become apprehensive when such a woman as yourself ventures beyond the safety zone.'

Serena regarded him curiously, moved by his frankness, and more disturbed than she cared to confess. 'You know something of the lot of white captives, then?'

'Too little, or too much.' He sighed. 'My brother was carried away—twenty years ago this month—by the Cheyennes. By now, he'll be a warrior with a dangle of white scalps at his belt.'

Again she felt a rush of sympathy, a confusing, almost startling surge of emotions. For the first time in many a day she was uncertain of her own impulses. It had seemed a stroke of luck when this man had turned up with a team and light wagon, on his way back to her own destination.

There had been the manifest hostility of Major O'Day, with his ugly insinuations, the warning of danger which O'Day had derided, and now these highly personal revelations.

'David,' she said, 'there are two kinds of men—and women: those who remain faithful, even to a memory—and the other kind. You cherish a memory. So do I. I was engaged to Lieutenant Sitterding. He was killed a year ago, next week.'

Moncur turned his head quickly, and his voice was rich with sympathy.

'Bob Sitterding? I met him two or three times. A fine officer, and a gentleman.'

'Thank you. But you understand—I hope. Neither of us—'

'Of course.' He nodded, and his simile was grave and warm. 'I'm honored by your confidence, Serena. And ahead's Fort

25

Lansing, at last. I anticipate the stir you'll make!'

CHAPTER THREE

Even in his imagination, with which he was so strongly gifted that at times it became a curse, Moncure had underestimated the excitement Serena would create. Not in a twelve-month had a new white woman arrived at Lansing, crouching remote and lonely in a land savagely beautiful and, as Dr. Karl Hochhalter had put it, beautifully savage.

It was even longer since one unattached and beautiful had cared or dared to make journey from that remote, almost forgotten country variously referred to as civilization, or home; a place where comforts were taken for granted, where security was not a nebulous thing watched and guarded by weary men on tireless patrol. All of them, from the lowliest foot soldier to Colonel Neilson, commanding, had known such a life, but memory had a way of fading even while it grew more poignant.

Serena Sullivan was the reincarnation of dreams, memories made real again. She came like a tonic, a sweeping wind and a shimmer of moonlight, and if the mixed simile was confused, it was at once clear to every man on the post, like the sudden breakthrough of sun long hidden behind a cloud.

Marcia, the colonel's lady, welcomed her with an unbelieving cry, while Myles Neilson himself looked half in wonder and half in disbelief from Moncure to his niece, his scowl lost in a broadening smile as he boomed a hearty welcome. The other officers appeared as though drawn by a magnet, finding urgent reasons to see the colonel, and as quickly forgetting them as they were dutifully introduced. The fort was bubbling and seething, as even word of imminent attack could not have stirred it.

Whether the inspiration came from the wives of the officers, or was the notion of the unmarried officers, plans for a gala welcoming ball were under way almost before Serena had time to refresh herself, or Moncure to enjoy his supper, badgered by the eager, envious questions of his fellows. Reasons for celebration were few enough at Fort Lansing, and no one could deny that the colonel's niece was reason enough.

'It will give every officer a chance to hold her in his arms, if only for a couple of turns around the floor,' Dr. Hochhalter observed, settling ponderously into a chair opposite Moncure and reaching automatically for the pot of coffee. They had been six weeks without a taste of the brew at Lansing; the supply trains had been twice attacked and half the contents destroyed. Moncure had

27

brought two full hundred-pound sacks of the beans up from Starke in the back of the wagon, and Karl Hochhalter loved his coffee.

'Ah!' He sighed, straining the black brew through the brush of cinnamon mustache, closing his eyes in brief ecstasy. 'Should I be about to die, now would be the moment, for truly I could say that I depart in peace!' He toyed with the empty cup. 'You are the envy of every young buck in camp, Dave, not to mention some of the older ones. And already they are planning the dance for Friday evening, and this is Tuesday already! That will give them time for preparations, if there's sufficient scurrying and scratching, and provided that the supply wagons which you report manage not only to survive but also to arrive.'

'The ball will take everyone's minds off their troubles,' Moncure observed.

'It will that, and be a better tonic than any I might concoct,' the doctor agreed. 'Also, it will be more tasty than sage and sulphur. It is a hero you are for bringing her—which will not deter a man of them from trying to beat your time with the lady. I trust that you improved each golden mile of the day?'

'It was a pleasant ride,' Moncure concurred, pushing back from the table, 'and all quite unexpected.'

'A pleasant ride, that man says, as though such journeys were commonplace! It is too bad that such an impulse to visit a relative does not occur more often to young ladies who are bored with the monotony of doing nothing.'

His manner changed abruptly. 'This wounded man, whom you took to my compatriot at Starke—it was Indians?'

'Who else could it have been?'

'Who, indeed? And they fled at your approach, not molesting you?'

'It sounds incredible,' Moncure admitted. 'I wouldn't have believed it.'

'There is medicine in the making,' Hochhalter observed, 'a dark and bitter brew, if I mistake not. Moreover, I have seen the moon of harvest rise blood red, with flames licking at the night sky!'

Having voiced his forebodings, he turned away, and Moncure stuffed his pipe carefully, enjoying the smoke in the softly closing dusk. They had been two months without tobacco, but he had brought a supply of that as well. They had not run short of vital supplies—ammunition for guns, beans and flour and soda—and more were on the way. But a man missed his pipe as he did his coffee. There were substitutes for both, each of which enhanced a man's delight in the genuine.

Life at Fort Lansing was not intended for pleasure, and there were few luxuries even for the married couples, to say nothing of the scarcity of necessities. Still and all, such a life had its compensations, its high moments, as now—

He approved of the ball. It would be a good thing, and pleasant; a break in the long monotony of days, each like all the others, though always spiced with surprise, the flavor of fear. His forbodings matched the doctor's; the smoke which rose and puffed and broke and vanished against the horizon, day after day, had the smell of suspense, the taint of terror.

It grew ranker in his own nostrils, despite the talk of peace, of the return of captives seized and held over the years, human chattels no less enslaved than the black men had been until a few years before, yet always with a difference. It was that difference which many well-wishers overlooked or chose to ignore, yet it was as vital as water to a man in the desert, as necessary as coffee to Karl Hochhalter.

There was talk of peace and the smoke of battle—battle joined only in remote skirmishes, at distant cabins and on lonely roads, bringing sudden yet terrible death; or the things worse than death—harbingers of evil to come, as surely as when the flocking birds flew southward, running from winter storm.

To his own knowledge, there were nearly a thousand red men of various tribes gathering across the plains, a preponderance being Cheyenne, since this was Cheyenne country. These were proud warriors, held in restraint by an uncertain treaty and the suspicious fear of such outposts as Starke and Lansing; restrained also by a lack of weapons with which to meet the hated white man on equal terms, and an age-old apprehension regarding other warriors of other tribes. They were fighters such as the Sioux and the Blackfoot and the Kiowa, the Crow and the Paiute and the Kansa.

Partly through skill and largely by luck, the white man had played them one against the other, thus holding in check tribes which, united, could have swept him from the land; hordes which might still join to do so, if fear and hatred of the pale-faced invader overcame their ancient animosities. If that day ever dawned—

Moncure knocked the dottle from his pipe, returning it to a pocket. For the moment it would be better to put such thoughts away as he did the pipe, firing them up only when the need arose. A man must have his moments of peace, relaxation to think of pleasant matters; else he would run naked into the storm, raving mad, as some had done. Now there was the ball—

'Captain Moncure? The colonel's compliments, sir, and he'd like a word with you.'

It was Slighbull Turner, the colonel's orderly, a precise young man with the habits of The Point still upon him. Moncure nodded and followed.

Myles Neilson was in his office, his chair shoved back from the cramping desk, his long legs outstretched. He waved Moncure to another chair, the hand holding his pipe weaving a small wreath of smoke with the gesture.

'I'd have had your report sooner, Dave, but you surprised me, as you did everyone,' he observed with a brief grin. An affection born of former association, of knowledge of each other's abilities, existed between them.

'Serena has told me how she happened to catch a ride with you, not entirely with Major O'Day's approval. But I'm curious as to how you happened to be at Starke at all.'

In the excitement of Serena's arrival, there had been no opportunity to go into detail about his scout, or to do more than mention the attack and the injured man. Now he reported with some care.

'I wondered where you got the wagon,' Neilson confessed. 'I jumped to the conclusion that Major O'Day must have supplied it, as faster and pleasanter transportation for my niece. Yet that was hard to credit. You believe it was Indians who made the attack?'

'I'm positive it was.'

Neilson, unlike O'Day, did not argue the point. 'It's odd that they failed to follow it up,' he mused. 'A man shot and helpless, and them hungry for hair . . . However, I have a dispatch here, among the mail which you brought. Orders to prepare for a meeting with the Indians of several different tribes, up at Hunk Gervais' outpost headquarters near Black Mountain.' Gervais was the Indian agent, the Cheyennes his particular charge. 'It appears that they have agreed to release all white captives.'

The thing had been in the wind for weeks, a rumor here, a whisper there. At first the men at Lansing refused to credit the talk as being more than rumor, a perennial bit of wishful thinking. Even now, after official confirmation, Moncure found it hard to believe.

'It could be the real thing,' he conceded doubtfully. 'Or it might be smoke in our eyes.'

Again, Neilson did not argue. He countered with another question.

'You found no guns?'

When setting out on the scout, it had occurred to Moncure that he might be able to stumble upon a cache of arms, hidden somewhere pending delivery to eager warriors. Many shreds of evidence had convinced them that modern rifles were being brought as contraband into the country, but solid proof was almost impossible to obtain.

Yet that such guns were reaching the Cheyennes, and in considerable numbers, Moncure was certain. How it was managed, and by whom, remained to be discovered. Unless the answer was found, their own destruction, there at Fort Lansing, as well as that of many other widely scattered across the border, was almost as inevitable as that the sun should set at day's end.

Such convictions seemed contradicted by the announced willingness of several tribes to meet with the white men and restore captives taken and held, some for long periods. Still, deception of the enemy was as old as warfare. The notable difference in this case seemed to be that it was conducted on a larger scale than usual, and more subtly.

'I didn't find any guns,' Moncure confessed, 'though I haven't seen any reason to change my mind about them . . . With your permission, I'll keep on searching.'

'If what we suspect is correct, then we'd better discover them while there's still time,' Neilson agreed grimly. 'Most others seem to be convinced that we're entering into an era of peace and good will, the dawn of the millennium. The report is that Little Wolf has consented with the rest.'

Little Wolf was the most dreaded and implacable war chief among the Cheyennes, a man compounded of myth and murder, yet grimly real. If he was involved in this . . .

'I wish I could feel some of that confidence.' Neilson made a wry face. 'Well, enough of that for tonight. My niece's sudden arrival has given everybody a big lift, and we certainly needed it.'

By the next morning, the garrison was in a ferment of excitement. Serena, looking as fresh as a prairie rose with the dew still upon it, despite the rigors of the previous day, greeted Moncure warmly. She looked faintly disappointed when it became evident that he was about to ride out again.

'You must be a man of iron,' she protested. 'Don't you ever get tired? I should think you'd want to rest a bit after the journey you've just made.'

'That turned into the biggest lift I've had in a long while,' Moncure assured her gallantly. 'This, as it happens, is to be only a short jaunt. Doctor Hochhalter has some sort of a theory which he's seeking to prove, and he invited me to accompany him.'

'Doctor Hochhalter? That's a German name, isn't it? And Moncure I take to be Welsh—certainly David Dunstan Moncure sounds that way. My uncle's is Neilson, and Scandinavian. Well, I'm only half-Irish,' she added brightly, 'so I guess I'm not entirely alien.'

'I suspect that you could easily find the opportunity to change your name,' Moncure observed dryly.

Serena colored faintly. 'I hope you have good luck on your quest.' For a moment her gaze revealed her anxiety. 'You and the Doctor are riding alone?'

'We shouldn't need any escort with all this talk of peace and good will,' he returned smiling. But the smile vanished once he and the short, heavy figure of the doctor were outside the compound. Karl Hochhalter filled his saddle like an overstuffed sack of feed grain.

'A beauteous lady,' the doctor commented. 'She comes like a memory of home to most of the men.'

'I hadn't realized that you were poetically inclined, Doctor.'

Hochhalter smiled. 'Poetry is not confined to words or rhyming or even to moonlight and roses . . . My apprehension is that she comes inopportunely.'

Colonel Neilson and Moncure had not discussed their fears with anyone, not even the dependable physician, but it was no surprise to Moncure that others should be apprehensive.

'What is it that you're looking for, Karl?'

'I'm not quite sure—yet,' Hochhalter acknowledged. His counter-question took Moncure by surprise. 'You told me once, if I remember correctly, that you had had the smallpox?'

'Yes, as a boy. I got off lightly.'

'So you did. No pock marks—and you are alive to tell of it. Not many are so fortunate. Well, we shall see.'

They had left the fort a dozen miles behind. He swung his horse toward a jumble of broken country where trees and clumps of brush relieved the monotony. Chokecherries blushed red in the sun, and wild yellow currants still made the mouth pucker, with the promise of honeyed ripeness just ahead, as Moncure pulled a few from a bush in passing.

All at once, hidden until that moment, a small trickle of water flowed dark in its shallow channel, issuing from under a cluster of boulders. Pitched nearby was an ancient-looking tepee. It seemed lonely and out of place, but Hochhalter clearly was not surprised.

'We white men—like all races, tribes and tongues—tend to feel superior, to look upon ourselves as more considerate of the welfare of others, less unselfish, than lesser breeds without the law,' he observed philosophically. 'That, I suppose, is a universal trait; actually, it is a far more common quality than is often realized.' He waved a hand toward the tepee.

'I rode this way a couple of days ago and was surprised, not to say intrigued, to discern a wisp of smoke off there. I investigated, and found this. It is occupied by an Indian—a

Cheyenne, Old Bear. Once, I believe, he was a warrior of considerable renown. Now he is old, and he approaches the end of the trail.

'During his lifetime, he has observed the effects of the white man's diseases upon his own people, who have scant resistance when unfamiliar plagues strike them. As proof of what I was just remarking, it occurred to Old Bear, when he felt the approach of sickness, that this illness might be different from the usual run, perhaps serious—one which could ravage his people.

'So he came here, far from the camp of his fellows, to set up his own tent and await the outcome. Should his sickness prove of no consequence, he could return in due course. But if it proved indeed a plague, then if he withdrew, the others might be spared. That much he told me, and I was moved by it, not having expected such philosophy or foresight from the man.'

Hochhalter dropped the bridle reins, dismounting heavily. Moncure followed.

Old Bear lay within the tent, stretched on a traditional robe of buffalo hide, and covered by a gaudily colored trade blanket. Tired eyes in a weary face rolled at their entrance, but he did not speak nor lift his head. The plague had about run its course, and that it was grave, Moncure saw only too plainly.

Presently they remounted their horses and rode away. Hochhalter had done what little

38

was possible, bringing fresh cold water in the earthen jar.

'He'll scarcely last out the day,' he observed. 'But he goes in peace, as becomes a warrior. Since he could not die in battle, he at least is able to do something for his people . . .

'Tomorrow I'll return with a shovel and bury him. At the same time, I'll burn the tepee and all its contents. With luck, his unselfish act may prove not to have been in vain. It all depends on whether or not he removed himself from among his companions in time, and, of course, on where he picked up the disease in the first place. If the plague should get started among a concentration of tribes—'

Though he left the thought unfinished, Moncure required no elaboration. Smallpox was devastating among red men. A prairie fire in dry grass was no more devouring.

'I will vaccinate everyone at the fort,' Hochhalter added. 'Fortunately, I suspected something like this, and was able to secure vaccine. Also, I have ordered more. Meanwhile, we can keep our fingers crossed!'

CHAPTER FOUR

Military discipline was undergoing a severe strain in the face of excited preparations for the ball. The wives of officers, rather than their husbands, were giving the orders, and the resultant chaos was akin to that caused by spring housecleaning. Despite what he had seen at the isolated tepee, Moncure was soon caught up in the contagion. Life was much like walking a tightrope, usually with a delicate balance maintained between tragedy and triumph.

The plague was not pleasant to contemplate—save that, should an epidemic start in spite of Karl Hockhalter and Old Bear, its decimating sweep through the tribes might solve other equally desperate problems.

Colonel Myles Neilson listened as they made their report, then signaled to Moncure to remain after Hochhalter had departed.

'You're going to hate me for what I have in mind,' he observed. 'But a report came in just before you fellows got back—a message from Major O'Day. I've no doubt that it gagged him to send it, after the things he'd said to you, but being a good military man, he did.

'Yesterday there was another murderous attack, not many miles west from where you and Serena were journeying. A stagecoach was carrying at least four passengers and the driver—all were murdered and scalped.

'As it happened, Lieutenant Atkinson, from Starke, was out on a scout with five men and a sergeant. Apparently they were not a great deal farther away, when the attack took place, than you had been the day before. They heard the commotion, including gunfire, though they were too far away to see what was happening. However, Mr. Atkinson lost no time in riding to the assistance of whoever might be under attack.' Neilson shrugged wearily.

'By the time they came up, it was too late for help. The Indians had fled at their approach, and since Mr. Atkinson estimated that his own party was badly outnumbered, he did not pursue. Sergeant Pryor informed him that they were Cheyennes. The lieutenant felt that his first attention should be for those who had suffered attack.

'They soon discovered that all were past their help. However, there was one oddity—which has given me an idea. In fleeing, the Indians appear to have overlooked one possible victim, who thus escaped losing his hair. The soldiers found him, crouching amid a clump of trees and brush, a quarter of a mile from the wrecked stagecoach. He was still upright, his back to a tree—without a scratch on him, but as dead as any of the others!'

'Heart failure,' Moncure commented.

'At least his heart had stopped. His belt had snagged against a broken stump of a limb, holding him up. Since he was a white man, and still warm, he was almost certainly one of the passengers from the stage. Sergeant Pryor's opinion was that the poor devil was literally scared to death.'

That might well be. Exertion and terror could kill as surely as bullets, given the proper combination of circumstances.

'Since the Indians had pulled out, they buried the victims, then hurried back to Fort Starke to report. Major O'Day was sufficiently shaken to dispatch reinforcements to guard the supply wagons which are on the road, and to hurry a report on here.'

In view of his own experience Moncure was hardly surprised. 'A bad business,' he observed.

'Very bad—particularly in view of these dispatches and orders which you brought me yesterday. Officially, a return of white captives from several different tribes had already been arranged and agreed to, and the news has spread, so that most people have relaxed their vigilance, confident that we are already entering upon an era of peace and good will. Actually, events seem to bear out our fears that all this is dust in our eyes.

'I don't need to remind you that it leaves us in a devil of a fix. We can't go out in force to disperse those who are gathering. They are only obeying orders, at least on the surface, and we'd bring down the vials of wrath upon our own heads—if we didn't get clobbered in the process. But guessing what they're up to isn't enough. We've got to be sure—and you know what that means.'

Moncure nodded. A conviction which satisfied themselves was not proof that would stand in the court of public opinion—or in a court-martial, should they be made the victims. On the other hand, dead men made poor witnesses.

'I've got a notion which may enable you really to find out what is going on, to get a look at the evidence,' Neilson went on. 'If you're eager to put your neck in a noose, that is, to see how it feels.'

'Nothing like trying it on for fit,' Moncure agreed.

'That extra dead man gave me the idea. For he got away—far enough, at least, to escape being killed in the attack; far enough to hide in the brush. So it's reasonable to suppose that the Indians either missed seeing him entirely, or assumed that he had escaped them for the time being. Perhaps they planned to hunt him down later—that would fit in nicely if it were so.'

Neilson took a turn up and down the room, then dropped back into his chair.

'Just suppose that such a man, lost and

43

apprehensive, but alive, should wander about the country for a matter of days, then stumble by chance into Hunk Gervais' far-back headquarters at Black Mountain? Do you see what I'm driving at?'

Moncure felt a quickening of excitement as he grasped the idea. Gervais was the Indian agent, and Neilson was admitting privately what he could not say publicly: that he mistrusted the man.

For such a mission, Moncure was the best, almost the only choice. Not only did he possess the requisite skill and background, but being new to Lansing, he and the agent were strangers one to the other.

There was not much doubt but that contraband was being supplied to the Indians, who were proving far from as friendly or placid as Gervais liked to picture them. The Indian agent had been a prime mover in the impending meeting of many tribes to effect the return of white captives.

'That meeting, when and if it takes place, is to be at Black Mountain,' Neilson added significantly.

Outwardly, the show of amity and the return of the captives was a development with much promise. It could also be a cover for incalculable mischief. The choice of Black Mountain for the get-together appeared more and more sinister.

Hunk Gervais' official headquarters were

within a comfortable distance of Fort Starke, and nothing untoward ever occurred there. It was at that lonely cabin near Black Mountain that he preferred to meet with his charges, maintaining what he termed a remote contact. Ostensibly, councils were held there, and supplies officially promised the Indians by government agreement or treaty were delivered.

Gervais' argument was that many of the more shy or suspicious Indians, who would refuse to venture near his headquarters, would meet him at so remote a spot.

'If such a missing man should stumble into his cabin—he might even be lucky enough to find out a few things, even see a few contraband guns,' Neilson added. 'Of course it's a risky business.'

'But promising,' Moncure agreed. 'I'll start tonight.'

Neilson looked pleased, then contrite.

'I thought you would,' he agreed. 'And I'm sorry as the devil about this, Dave. You deserve a chance to rest. Worse, this will make you miss the ball, which is too bad.'

'With such a stray man wandering about, time is important,' Moncure said, swallowing his disappointment. After all, he'd had a day with Serena along the road.

'You'll ride halfway there?' Neilson suggested. 'Then you can hide your horse and go the rest of the way on foot.'

45

'It would be difficult to conceal a horse in that section of country,' Moncure pointed out. 'Also, if I walk all the way, it will be more convincing.'

The moon had risen when he stepped out from his quarters, attired, as the missing man had been, in not too new Levis and down-at-the-heel boots. The transformation from the officer who had ridden with Doctor Hochhalter was subtle but definite.

His life, as well as the success of his mission, might well hinge upon the skill with which he played his part. It was his hope not only to surprise the agent in the act of pulling a double-cross, but perhaps to find still more. Luck always played a part, but skill and experience also counted heavily.

Most activity at the fort had ceased, save for the planning by the woman. Bright lights in the Neilson home testified that details were still being discussed.

He had to pass it on his way to the gate. As he approached, a shimmering figure in white drifted toward him, almost ethereal under the moonlight. Moncure caught his breath, staring in amazement. Serena was looking with equal surprise at his attire, the evident preparations for departure.

'I stepped outside for a last breath of air before retiring,' she explained. It had been a hot day; the sun had beat down relentlessly. 'The ladies—bless their excitement—finally decided that there would be another day tomorrow. You aren't leaving again, David—already?'

'I'm afraid so,' Moncure replied, and doffed a weathered and shapeless hat. 'Something has come up.'

The quick anxiety in her eyes did not escape him. Some of her apprehension spilled into her voice.

'If you must go in such guise, then of course it will be dangerous. Will you be gone long?'

'A matter of a few days, most likely,' he explained. 'I'll be sorry to miss the dance. I was looking forward to it.'

'So was I. I had intended to save both the first and last dances for you. Such others as you obtained, you would have to ask for,' she added archly. Then the pretense fell away. That she was on the verge of saying more he was sure, but she remembered that he was a soldier, and she a soldier's daughter. She smiled instead.

'There will be other times.'

'There will, indeed,' he promised. 'Good night, Serena.'

'Good night—David,' she said, and this time the catch in her breath betrayed her. 'You go alone?'

'That's the way it has to be.'

'Then—God go with you.'

While they talked, Moncure had been

aware of Sergeant Hauswitz, checking his stride and watching from a respectful distance. Now he advanced with the portentous gait of a drillmaster.

'Excuse me, Cap'n, but I couldn't help overhearing that one remark, and I don't like it—you going alone. And not even in uniform,' he added disapprovingly. 'It ain't quite right, sir.'

'But it's best,' Moncure returned. 'Good night, Sergeant.'

'Good night, Cap'n, sir, and—it ain't usually my way, but I hope you won't take it amiss, sir, if I should say a few words for your well-being in a prayer this night, sir.'

'I'll take it kindly, Sergeant. As Miss Sullivan reminded us, we do not ride alone.'

That was a comforting thought to hold onto, and as he moved out through the gate and watched it swing shut behind him, he had need of such comfort.

CHAPTER FIVE

Moncure shook his head, irritated with himself. What had she said the other afternoon about the faithful and those who were not? He still counted himself an engaged man, pledged to a lovely woman.

Still, it was hard to pretend, knowing what
48

he did. A year was a long time, and two of them stretched out like an age. For a captive, under such conditions—

His sigh choked on hopelessness, a strangled sob tearing from his heart. There was no one to see or hear.

He walked until the moon dipped below the horizon, then slept. There was no sure way of knowing whether or not he had been watched, but he doubted it, and on that supposition he was staking the success of this trip, perhaps his life. For the most part the Indians kept the fort under observation. That was known. But they watched from a long way back, as suited their purpose. It would require sharp eyes to spot a lone man at midnight.

He took his time the next morning, moving clumsily, uncertainly. Should he be seen, he was an aimless wanderer, lost in a wide land.

Wide it was, and lonely. This was Cheyenne country, an empire of broken plain and rolling hills, with far-spaced clumps of brush or trees; an open land, yet with terrain in which armies might lie concealed, squads of the scarlet cavalry of the plains, who were among the finest horsemen and fighters the world had produced.

Once he saw buffalo grazing in the distance, the rear guard of a fair-sized herd, moving away at an untroubled pace. The land had a deceptive look of emptiness. There was also a growing sense of familiarity.

He hadn't been sure whether he would remember or not. Years could play tricks on the mind, even if the terrain remained unaltered. It was a long while since he'd been in that part of the country, for he hadn't scouted there since coming to Fort Lansing. Yet these unmistakably were the scenes of his early boyhood.

This was the same mighty sweep of country which had held so powerful an attraction for his father a score of years earlier. George Moncure had been driving a wagon on the Oregon trail, the rich lands of the Willamette his goal. Instead, he'd turned aside, drawn by the immensity of these plains, the promise whispered in the wind. He hadn't worried about the Indians, or unduly about his family. It had always been his boast that he could live on friendly terms with any neighbors, whatever the color of their skin.

For a time it had worked. He'd built his cabin, cutting a patch of timber, hauling the logs and erecting them by dint of much sweat and strain. Moncure had been a small boy, but he remembered some of that life, which now seemed more like a dream than reality.

It had been real enough when the raiders struck. He topped a slope and looked down at the little valley, green in memory, green now with the rich grass of summer. Before his eyes was the house, or what remained of it—rotting, blackened embers of logs, half-hidden in the luxuriant growth, all that remained of hopes long since as dead as those who had died amid the ruins. . . .

At the time of the attack, he had been wandering on the hillside, a small boy playing games, and the game had suddenly become reality before his eyes. He'd crouched shivering amid the brush for the remainder of the day, and the long night which followed. He had ventured out only when a party of neighbors, from miles away, had arrived fearfully to investigate and to bury the dead . . .

Some day he'd visit those forgotten graves, but not now. It could ruin everything to turn aside, if he was being watched.

He kept on, his apparently aimless way leading toward a definite destination. There had been an added reason to make this trip now, while opportunity beckoned. Another scout, official in buckskin, had reported a wagon was heading for Black Mountain. Ostensibly it carried regulation government supplies for the Indians, but he'd been suspicious that the real cargo was rifles.

It had been impossible to confirm that guess, but it was a lead worth checking, especially when half a hundred rifles, or the lack of them, might win a battle or lose a war. They might even prevent a war from erupting in all its fury, should he manage right and have a bit of luck.

Luck was always a vital ingredient, but a man could make his own, to a certain extent.

The sun was growing hot. He swung toward a grove of trees, half hidden in a draw. There should be water, and here streams were far apart.

He rounded the trees before he saw it—the charred remains of hope, where luck had played out. After a score of years, the pattern had changed but little. Here had stood another cabin, half soddie, half log, not long before. Some settler, prospector or trapper, had gambled and lost.

The Indians had been there, perhaps a week before. There was a spring, and Moncure had his drink. The sun was hidden by a drift of cloud, and the day grew more somber as he went on.

Eyes might be observing him from close at hand, or the land might be as empty as it looked. Traveling in this fashion, it was impossible to be sure.

Today there was no smoke rising high; nothing to fill the empty space but hope and doubt.

His nose detected a stench drifting on the wind and gave warning before his eyes. Somewhere to the east was the South Branch, and off there Black Mountain reared, a gnarled thumb against the sky. Closer, as though lining the mountain, spidery

52

platforms set high on rickety-seeming poles reared in their turn above the earth. It was their burden which diffused the stench.

Moncure studied them, keeping well away. It was an Indian burial plot—you could scarcely call it an Indian burial ground, for the Cheyenne, unless death came overwhelmingly, buried their people high in the air, wrapping them in skins and blankets. They tied the bodies, well bundled, on the platforms atop the poles.

On certain occasions, the relatives of the deceased would come, the mournful squaws wailing, bearing offerings for the dead: food, sometimes arms, gifts or trinkets useful for the long journey toward the happy hunting grounds.

Otherwise, no one ever approached such a place—no one save a fool or an enemy.

Such burial groves, if that was a proper term for the man-made trees, were sacred, the resting places of the dead. Woe to any who trespassed or desecrated them.

Moncure had no intention of doing either. He preferred to keep as far away as possible, though he noticed that this was a bigger plot than most, with many buried there, apparently over a long span of time.

Aside from the poles and their burdens, the land hereabouts lay stark and empty. The ground was hard, rocky, and the grass scanty. For miles there was no draw, no coulee, no hiding place, it seemed, even for a jackrabbit.

Yet not far off, somewhere at the somber foot of the Black Mountain, was his destination. There, with luck, he might find what he was looking for, possibly even obtain a break which could prevent a war.

Despite the emptiness, he had the feeling that hordes lay in wait, as well they might. Off beyond Black Mountain was a massive, ragged canyon, cradling a river as dark as the mountain. Along the canyon were hiding places for a score of tribes, if they wished to use them.

Not that they would bother to hide now. It was here that the tribes were supposed to gather, to palaver and finally to return captives held over the years. Some of the tribes might already be arriving.

Moncure knew the history of those which the soldiers watched and tried to control. There were the Pawnees and the Cheyenne, who for most of the century had been friends in a wary sort of fashion, then, no longer than a year or so before, had been poised, ready to spring at one another's throats. It had been a matter of sacred medicine arrows, daringly stolen by a handful of rival warriors. Powerful medicine was always greatly to be desired, so that risks could be taken. But such stealing had been almost as taboo as desecration of the graves of the dead.

Even so, there had been no war. Instead

there had been a powwow, with one tribe paying a stiff price in ponies for the return of the medicine arrows. Thus peace, rent and torn, had been papered over. It was an indignity which must still rankle, but matters which even half a decade earlier would have caused intertribal wars were now overlooked, because of a matter far more grave and vital.

While the great war between the white men had continued, the Indian had enjoyed a sort of breathing spell. Now that that struggle was fading even in memory, new hordes of settlers were pushing west, threatening the lands, the life, the very existence of every tribe. So hate was smoldering, and erstwhile friends were turning against the white men.

Already, warriors of other remote tribes had been seen by the scouts in the vicinity—braves of the Arapaho, emissaries from the Sioux. The possibility that many tribes might unite for a sudden devastating war against all whites caused men's hair to gray prematurely.

One thing, Moncure was positive, had delayed such a strike. That was the need for more guns; modern weapons, as good or better than the ones the soldiers possessed. Now, from all accounts, they were getting such guns, doing it under the talk of peace and the return of captives. That made an almost perfect smoke screen.

Even such a monster as Black Mountain

was slow to grow against the sky, yet it loomed big. In that clear high air distances were deceiving; objects a score of miles away seemed almost at hand. It was late in the afternoon when he saw the cabin and the canyon beyond, the mountain dwarfing both.

This was a soddie, with a door of rough-hewn planks. A small twist of smoke climbed from a pipe thrust through the roof. Its appearance was so peaceful and at variance with the surroundings that it was hard to believe there was anything sinister about it.

This was the outpost favored by the Indian agent, well away from easy observation by the soldiers or others who might grow overly curious. Here, whether due to good management or otherwise, Gervais went among his charges without fear or hindrance. That was not to be wondered at, since he also distributed the largesse, or what passed for that, of the Great White Father.

Stumbling to the door, Moncure halted, with an entirely genuine sigh of relief. He rattled the catch, and a man opened it, squinting against the declining sun.

Shock coursed through Moncure, and it was an effort to keep his face impassive. Here, at a moment when he had least expected it, he was at the end of a long trail.

The agent was short and rolypoly in build, whereas Dr. Hochhalter, equally squat and heavy, was square, almost wedge-shaped.

56

Whiskers as golden as the sun covered the agent's face, and his eyes glinted bluely from under thicket-thick eyebrows. Only his nose spoiled the almost cherubic effect, being both bulbous and purple.

Unless Moncure was badly mistaken, this was the man he had vainly sought for years, the head of the ring who had always managed to elude him, finally vanishing like one of the wisps of smoke against the horizon.

Any doubt that plotting and intrigue were going on here was gone. This man was a past master at deviltry. And if Gervais should suspect Moncure's identity in turn—

Apparently he did not. This was their first face to face encounter, and the seedy-looking individual hardly resembled a colonel of cavalry. An emotion of pity and solicitude transformed Gervais' face as Moncure told his story, nor did Moncure doubt the genuineness of his emotion. Though a master at murderous planning on a large scale, Hunk Gervais personally was like a kindly old uncle.

'What in the world—why, what have we here? Come in, man, come in!' Taking Moncure's arm, he assisted him to a thick pile of buffalo skins in a corner of the cabin, where he sank down with a sigh. 'You're all played out. Here, take a pull at this. It should help.'

He produced a flask, twisting the cork from

it and tendering it. Moncure swallowed a gulp of the fiery liquor, gasped, and shook his head.

'Thanks,' he managed. 'My name's Leafelt. I never expected to find a white man livin' back in here. I'd just about given up hope of ever finding anything again.'

'You appear to have come a long way,' Gervais observed. 'As a matter of fact, I do not live here. My name is Gervais, Mr. Leafelt. I am the Indian agent, and sometimes transact business from this remote outpost.'

Moncure blinked, taking time to digest what he had heard before speaking again. His head-shake was wondering.

'It's a near miracle, just the same,' he whispered. 'I've been walking, wandering—for days, I guess. I've kind of lost track of time. I knew I was lost, but I had to keep going. When I saw a cabin off here, I could hardly believe it was real.'

'You're among friends now,' Gervais soothed him. 'Such an experience, I know, can be soul-shaking. But what happened, if you're not too tired to tell me? Did you lose your horse?'

'I never had a horse. I was with others on the stage, headin' east when all at once we were jumped by Indians, a lot of them. It was terrible. They were like a lot of devils, swarming around with no warning at all.

58

Everybody else was killed. Somehow I got off into some deep brush, and they missed me. After it got dark, I started to walk, tryin' to follow the road, but I guess I lost it in the night—'

In general detail his story matched the true story of what had happened two or three days before, and he had no doubt that the report of it would have reached Gervais. His appearance corroborated his story. Sympathetically, Gervais helped him remove his boots, clucking as Moncure showed feet swollen from much walking. Apparently the sight dissipated such lingering doubts as he might have entertained.

'Your story, sir, would be difficult to credit, did not your condition speak for itself. What you say about an attack on a stagecoach is news, and I must confess myself shocked as well as horrified. I cannot imagine what venturesome braves would have done such a thing, though it becomes understandable, since many different tribes are converging on this section—with peaceful intentions, of course. However, wild ones cannot always resist temptation. Many have never enjoyed more than the most cursory contact with civilization.'

His tone grew brisk.

'Your ordeal is over. Lie back and rest, Mr. Leafelt. I'll rustle you up something to eat. You must be starved.'

There was a fireplace in one corner of the cabin, a table and pile of sacks and boxes, and a couple of bunks against one wall. Moncure noticed that one of the bunks was occupied, its occupant peering slyly over the top. The agent set about preparing a meal, and Moncure was more than willing to stretch out on the buffalo skins.

During the course of an apparently aimless conversation, Gervais drew Moncure's story from him in greater detail, again shaking his head over the account of the attack.

'I sincerely hope and trust that all such episodes may soon be a thing of the past. As it is, you are very fortunate to be alive—more lucky than you know.'

'I realize that,' Moncure agreed. 'Specially lucky to find you here, when I was at the end of my rope. Though what I'll do now, I don't rightly know. I've lost everything—'

'You still have your life,' Gervais reminded him. His eyes were speculative. 'Set up and eat now. Then get a good sleep tonight. As for something to do, it's just possible that I may be able to find a job for you. Your coming at this particular time may be providential for me also.' He jerked a thumb toward the bunk.

'Maybe you've noticed Old Sam there. He's been my right-hand man in this country, chiefly because he knows how to get along with Indians. It's not everybody can do that.

As I told you, there is to be a big gathering of several tribes in this vicinity, and we are here to prepare for that. There are a thousand things to do, and as ill luck would have it, Sam's horse threw him yesterday, and he broke his leg. Which leaves me short-handed at a critical time.'

'That's too bad,' Moncure sympathized. 'If there's anything I can do to help, to show my appreciation, I'll sure try.'

'I think there may be. There's one job that needs immediate attention—delivering a load of garden tools to some of my charges. Can you drive a team?'

'I've worked around horses all my life,' Moncure replied truthfully.

'Excellent. In that case, you can do that tomorrow. It will benefit both of us at the same time.' Carefully selecting a tuft of whisker, he tugged thoughtfully at it. Moncure took notice, for this was an identifying trait of the man he had sought so long.

'Ordinarily I would hesitate to assign a newcomer to such a task. Of course it's really not difficult, and there will be no danger as long as you follow instructions. You will be dealing with my particular charges, the Cheyennes, and so long as they understand that you are working for me, there will be no trouble. I call them my people, and I am proud to say that they give me their trust.

61

'On the other hand, Indians are still children of nature, and as such, they are quick to resent anything which smacks of disloyalty. What I am trying to point out, for your protection as well as mine, is that if anyone should be so foolish as *not* to do a job as he was supposed to, then they would be down on him like a hawk on a gopher.'

CHAPTER SIX

Having delivered this not too oblique warning against the possible temptation of disloyalty, Gervais became the perfect host. He left the pile of skins for Moncure, while he occupied the other bunk.

With daylight, Moncure could make out the outlines of tepee villages, set up along the rim of the canyon. Though barely visible, they were proof that the tribes were already assembling. With the land swarming with warriors who would do the agent's bidding, Gervais had evidently concluded that he ran no risk in entrusting a possibly delicate chore to a newcomer. A single misstep would bring them down on Moncure, as his simile had put it, like a hawk on a gopher.

Again that morning, Gervais' humor proved rough and ready, as soon as breakfast was out of the way.

'You've really been lucky, Leafelt, stumbling around aimlessly and still getting this far. Fool's luck, one might term it. You could easily have been planted by now—always providing for the long chance that anybody happened along who would take the trouble to dig a grave. That supposition sort of makes you a planter, doesn't it—and me with this load of garden tools crying to be delivered!' He shook with laughter, golden beard and round belly shaking in unison.

'Yes, planting is an apt word for it. It is also something that I've been talking about and working toward, as an agent, for a long time. Finally we are making a start. Let me show you.'

Half concealed by a clump of brush was a light wagon, similar to the one in which Moncure had journeyed a few days before. It was already loaded with long wooden boxes, covered by a scrap of tarp. Tugging this back, Gervais' gesture was as blandly disarming as his words.

'Garden tools. Plain, old-fashioned hoes and rakes and spades. Those boxes could fool a man, if he didn't know better, into thinking maybe they held guns, but he'd be dead wrong. And in this country, being wrong is a synonym for being dead. Here; I'll show you.'

Catching up a hammer and chisel from the bottom of the wagon box, he loosened the top

63

board of one of the boxes to reveal the contents.

'These are for my charge, the Cheyennes. There are none for any of the visiting tribes, of course, though I trust that may be arranged later. And do you know, sir, even with all the excitement of this unprecedented gathering of many tribes, my people are as excited as a bunch of children about these tools! They have been looking forward to them with a fervor approaching that of some other tribes seeking the white man's Book of Heaven!

'At first, when I got the idea, it required almost as much talking and persuading to convince the government that the idea might be sound, and to get them to send these tools, as it did to talk the Indians into wanting to learn a new way of life. But I pride myself that I can be persuasive when I set out to be, and I do take a fatherly interest in the welfare of my people. If we are to take away their fighting and hunting, they must have something to take its place, something new and different. What could be better than to raise a crop which they can eat?'

The argument was plausible-sounding, at least on the surface. Dubiously, Moncure suggested a flaw.

'Ain't it kind of late in the season to be starting a garden? Not much time left for growing a crop.'

64

'You're right about that,' Gervais agreed readily. 'The fault, however, is not mine. It took various underlings back at headquarters so long to get moving that the tools and garden seeds have been unnecessarily delayed. They have, in fact, just arrived. But my charges know that they are on the way, and they have been looking forward to them with the same expectancy with which a child anticipates Santa Claus. So, now that they have come, I can't hold them back. Besides, if they prepare the ground, spading and making ready, it will insure a better crop next year.'

He replaced the lid on the box; then they harnessed a team and hitched it to the wagon. Gervais gave particular directions on his destination.

'You will have to drive for most of the day. See that little spike of butte, off to the west? Head for it. When you approach it, you will find a creek. Although the country thereabouts is quite flat, there are a couple of knolls right alongside the stream. You can't miss them. Stop when you reach them. No doubt some of the Indians will be waiting for you. If not, they will soon show up.

'They know this team and wagon, and will understand what it is that you will bring, even if you can't talk their language. Knowing that you represent me, they will treat you well. Turn the boxes over to them;

65

then return here tomorrow. That's all you have to do. But I must caution you to do no tampering with anything, as that might make them suspicious. I would regret it if you should have any unnecessary trouble.'

Moncure had no doubt as to what the other boxes held. The one did contain garden tools, but that was to show such men as himself. In the others would be rifles—at least half a hundred, assembled and ready for use. Undoubtedly there was ammunition, many rounds for each rifle, also packed in the boxes.

He could verify his suspicions by having a look, and once it was safe, he intended to do so. The perplexing question now was what to do with his find. Luck, and being at the right place at the right time, had brought an important discovery. It also posed a problem.

By following directions, he could deliver the guns without rousing suspicion, winning the trust both of the agent and the Indians. That, for the moment at least, would assure his own safety. He could return and report to Colonel Neilson, with sufficient evidence to take action against the agent and perhaps stop a further flow of forbidden arms.

That would be the safest course, but not necessarily the best. For it would assure the delivery of these modern guns to warriors already near the brink of revolt. Their possession might well tip the scale. Even if it

66

did not, that many additional guns could well spell victory or defeat in a later battle, one in which the men from Fort Lansing would almost surely be involved.

To prevent the delivery of the guns was of first importance. Yet at the moment, driving as directed toward the distant spire, he could see no feasible solution.

The land still looked empty, but if he swung the team toward Fort Lansing and put the horses to as fast a pace as they could maintain, watchful eyes would be quick to notice the change in direction. Within an hour, he would be surrounded by an angry horde. Even if he escaped with his life, they'd have the guns.

The only other alternative was to hide them somewhere, then take a chance on delivering boxes still closed but filled with stones of equal weight, packed in such fashion as not to rattle. By showing a decoy box, with a layer of rifles on top when it was opened, that might possibly be contrived. If he was lucky, he might manage it and still escape with his life.

The difficulty was in deciding how to make the substitution, and where and how to cache the rifles, so that they would not be found once the deception was discovered. Even should he prove to be a spy, Gervais was counting on the open plain and watchful eyes to thwart any possible counter-move. It would be folly to run the risk, unless Moncure had reasonable assurance that the cached guns would remain concealed until he could lead a troop of soldiers to the hiding place.

As always, the wide sweep of the land appeared deserted, empty. Today there were no buffalo anywhere in sight, no moving life of any kind. Far to the west, where the guiding butte reared, a few puffs of smoke arose lazily, hanging, dissolving against the horizon. That was a signal to eager warriors that the wagon and the promised guns were on the way.

Otherwise there was nothing to see. But should he stop for long and try to find a hiding place, it would be noted. The companion problem was equally perplexing. Even if he could work unobserved, where in that open country could he find a hiding place which would not quickly be spotted?

Indians were notoriously sharp-eyed, adept at reading sign. Anything that he did had to be done well.

It was somewhat puzzling that the guns were to be delivered at a point so remote even from the outpost, but that might be the answer. Great care was being taken, at this stage of the game, to do everything to avoid possible discovery by any of Colonel Neilson's scouts.

Ten days before, the sweep of grass had

been studded with a rainbow carpet of wild flowers. Their blossoms had vanished, and the grass held straight in the face of the sun, bending to the wagon wheels but soon lifting again once they had passed.

That was unusual. Normally there was wind across these wastes. The absence of even a tempering breeze suggested an oncoming storm. Moncure scanned the sky hopefully. There was not even a handful of cloud to mar the sweep of blue.

The sky was the guileless hue of Hunk Gervais' eyes, and a more guileful man had never crossed Moncure's path. Here, too, storm could come up fast, and the feel of it was in the air. Possibly, should a storm come, with a cover of rain and a buffeting gale, he might be able to conceal the rifles—if he could find some adequate place in which to cache them.

His course was taking him partly back over ground which he had covered the day before. He allowed the horses to pick their own pace. There was no outward reason for haste. Garden tools or rifles might be eagerly awaited, but it was already months too late for a crop this year.

Hunk Gervais, Indian agent. After all, it was not surprising to find him in a position of such influence and responsibility. The man was clever, greatly daring. Moncure had known him as Oldhouse, but that too was

69

probably not his name. What mattered, with massive trouble brewing on the border, was that Oldhouse was involved, directing a plot before which even his own previous efforts seemed petty.

All at once the wind came, freshening sharply, and clouds grew like the breath of a released genie, piling in the northeast. If Moncure knew anything about weather, there would be a slashing shower by early afternoon. Following several rainless days, turbulence was to be expected.

He halted the wagon, allowing the horses a breather. Working swiftly, he examined another box. As he had been sure would be the case, the tools revealed were those of destruction, not intended for digging a garden.

A look at the rifles was revealing. As he had expected, these were the latest model, better guns than either North or South had possessed during the years of war, equipment superior to that provided the garrisons at Lansing or Starke. Guns which could turn the tide of war, in the hands of enemies.

R. Savage had turned out more than two million rifles for the Union armies, or at least the Northern arsenals had manufactured variations of his .58 caliber. At war's end, a variation had again been devised, to make breechloaders out of the previous models by introducing a hinged breech block in front of the hammer.

But these guns were the '66 model, center-fire rather than rimfire, the caliber reduced from .58 to .50 by brazing a tube inside the barrel and then rifling it. Soberly Moncure clucked to the horses.

Off to the side but out of sight were the ruins of his boyhood home. His jaw clamped. This one shipment must contain five dozen rifles, of a quality which could decide a war. Such a war would strike swiftly, devastatingly, at other such scattered cabins, as though there had been no lapse of years, no palaver of peace.

From the Indians' point of view, they were hardly to be blamed. Now that the big war was over, impoverished families were migrating west in constantly increasing numbers, seeking free land, a chance to start over. The pressure against the Indian and his mainstay of life, the buffalo, was becoming unbearable. For him, it was a case of fight or perish.

What he could not envision was that those hordes out of the east were too great to be checked by fire or famine, flood or pestilence, by the arrow by day or the terror by night. The day of the red man was drawing to an end, at least according to the sort of life which he had known, and nothing could change that. Only the degree of blood letting could be affected, and it was the Army's business to protect the settlers, to hold carnage to a minimum.

Moncure studied the building rim of clouds. Off to the side, a few miles ahead, reared the poles of the burial place in the sky. Today the symbolism was unpleasantly grim.

A thought buzzed like a mosquito at the rim of his consciousness, just out of reach and therefore annoying, refusing either to come within grasping distance or to go away. The wind came with a rush, bursting with a violence compounded of elemental forces too long held in check. The sky darkened like the blowing out of a lamp.

This would be no gentle summer shower, no casual storm. The land had grown thirsty, lying overlong in the hungry sun. The drenching it was about to receive might prove prolonged and savage, but that was the way of nature, which took on the characteristics of the country.

He could see the burdened poles, leaning, swaying to the push of the wind. Normally they withstood whatever pressures might be exerted, and they would probably do so again. Like Moncure and the horses, they had no choice. Everything that could was scurrying for shelter. A jackrabbit raced past in giant leaps; birds strove against the buffeting wind. Uprooted clumps of sage tumbled with giant swings.

Moncure had it then, the idea which had

eluded him but now stung like a wasp. It was a notion so wild that he rejected it out of hand as impossible. Then he fell to considering it, a sweating excitement mounting in him to the accompanying tempo of the storm. The notion was fantastic, probably unworkable; nonetheless it loomed as a possibility, the only chance available.

Should he make the attempt and fail, his life would be forfeit, and horribly so. He could picture clearly the sort of vengeance which the enraged Indians would inflict upon him before finally allowing death to come to his rescue. The explosion of their rage might even trigger the general attack against which he strove to guard.

Against such hazards were the very real risks that the guns might fall into the hands of glory-hungry braves, already teetering on the brink of open warfare. The newly burnt hut he had come upon the day before, the recent attacks, were straws in the wind. Against that danger, and the added murderous potential which these guns would give, he could not weigh personal risks.

Suddenly the clouds were all around, shutting away the horizon, slashed by lightning which raced at them with giant leaps. Its rumble brought uneasy snorts from the horses. Moncure made up his mind, swinging the team about.

Though the distance had been halved, he

could no longer see the poles which reared against the horizon. But that meant, too, that no distant watchers could see him. The first drops of rain came spattering as he pulled the horses to a halt. Here was one more chance which had to be taken; the chance that he was near enough, yet not too close. There was no time to waste in searching, yet to be either too close or too far away could ruin everything.

Hereabouts the ground was hard and rocky, and the grass sparse. On such terrain neither hoofs or wheels would leave much sign, even after heavy rain. Still he dared not approach too closely, for his sign might be discovered, and that was to be avoided at all costs.

Yet if he were too far away he would have an impossibly burdensome task, with too little time in which to do it. Jumping down, he unhooked the traces, tying one horse to a wagon wheel. Then he turned his attention to prying open the boxes. All save the decoy were loaded with rifles.

By now the storm was across the land, lashing with all its threatened fury. The wind made him gasp and stagger, and the slash of rain was creating sudden pools and rivulets. Picking up as many rifles as he could carry, he headed in what he hoped was the proper direction. It was impossible to see.

He had always had an instinct for finding his way, even in the dark of night, and that was with him now. The graveyard in the sky was off at the side, as he had judged. The burdened poles groaned and creaked, swaying in the wind; loose ends of hides and blankets, which wrapped the mummified bodies, streamed and snapped in the gale.

The air was washed, the stench of decay whipped away. A pole, leaning somewhat, afforded a chance to climb. The buffeting storm added to the difficulty of his task, making the poles slippery, hard to cling to. He worked in a sort of frenzy, hoisting himself and the rifles, stuffing them among the wrapped skins and blankets. They were shoved out of sight, around, above and below the bodies of warriors long dead, and some not so long in the happy hunting grounds.

Somehow he managed, retracing his steps at a stumbling run, returning, laden again, and repeating the process in a frenzy of haste and fatigue. It was necessary to climb to several different graves, and some were difficult to attain. More than once he faltered, on the verge of exhaustion, then kept on doggedly.

Finally there was only the ammunition, the boxes of shells. These also must cached, hidden where no one would think to look, and they presented a special problem.

When he was able to pause, the storm was beginning to slacken, though still casting a gray veil over the plain. The storm had endured for an hour, and he'd needed every desperate minute. If the rain would continue a little while longer, it would be his salvation.

Rearranging the boxes in the wagon, he hooked up the team and drove on. Most sign would be washed away. At least he hoped so.

He drove for a mile, and found the wind was gone, the rain no more than a drizzle. Here was another stretch of rocky ground, where the stones were not merely embedded, but where there was much loose rock ready at hand.

Stopping again, he took what he needed, selecting only stones whose absence would go unnoticed by any save the sharpest eyes. When the boxes were filled with a heavy load, he nailed the lids shut again. One box was arranged with guns on top. Another had the garden tools exactly as before. The other boxes were piled below.

As he drove on again, the clouds began to lift and the sun to burst through, reasserting its lordship. The land lay washed and freshened, and his deeds had been covered as effectively as by darkness.

So far, he was well satisfied with his day's work, with the whole expedition. There would still be risk when he delivered the boxes, for over-eager warriors might get out of control and discover the deception.

Otherwise, it was unlikely that anyone would suspect the hiding place he had chosen for the guns. The burial place was unthinkable, ground too sacred ever to approach lightly. Except when additional bodies were brought, only squaws came out. They ventured fairly close on occasion, bringing offerings for the departed and wailing for the dead, but even they rarely did more than look upon the elevated graves from a distance.

The rain had washed away his sweat, and as his breathing returned to normal, Moncure was able to grin. He suspected that even the best scouts of the tribe might be in for some perplexing days when they found stones substituted for guns, and searched the limitless plains for a cache no longer on earth.

CHAPTER SEVEN

In the lands bordering the Mississippi, the aftermath of such a downpour would be mud and lingering pools for several days. Here in Cheyenne country, water drained away almost as swiftly as it came, and the eager sun in high light air, reasserting its mastery, left a patina of dry ground by the time Moncure sighted the twin knolls. Here, for the first time since he had left Lansing, was activity. A tepee had been pitched near the bank of the creek, apparently to serve as temporary

77

headquarters for the agent's agent. In and around the neighborhood loitered at least a score of Indians, all warriors, who observed the approach of the wagon with unconcealed interest.

This, of course, was a trading deal. As representative of the Great White Father, Hunk Gervais might dispense treaty goods with a lavish hand, but the running of contraband was something else. Rifles were forbidden, and Hunk expected to be well paid for taking advantage of his position to betray his government.

Thus the tepee became, in a sense, a trading post. Moncure studied the setup with wry approval. The reason for all these shadowy procedures was obvious. Not even at the cabin by Black Mountain did the agent care to risk completing the transaction. The man he had secured to take the guns a long day's haul beyond that point was a down-at-the-heels stranger. Should anything go wrong, Hunk Gervais could disclaim any responsibility. Gervais was too canny to show up here to conclude the deal. An underling was entrusted with that task.

No one interfered as he drove up and stopped. The sun was setting in a splash of glory, dusk following hard at his heels. Everything had been well timed, according to instructions. By morning, the pre-agreed terms of the barter would have been finished, the rifles distributed, and the newly proud owners scattered beyond discovery. The wagon, laden with furs, would be ready to return.

A saddled horse was tethered in the brush, just behind the tepee. Moncure eyed the saddle. Undoubtedly this animal belonged to the trader.

The man who emerged from the tepee was easy to classify: A squaw man. Such existence put its stamp upon a man. He was not at all the same as a white captive turned Indian, in whom pride burned high and fierce. The average squaw man had left pride behind, exchanging his heritage for the doubtful ease of an existence which never quite became a way of life.

This man was tall, almost effetely handsome. Probably his good looks had been his curse. His indifferent slouch did not conceal the anticipation in his eyes.

'You got the tools?' he asked.

'Right here,' Moncure agreed. 'Had kind of a wet ride.' He wrapped the reins about the brake rod, though the tired team would have stood, glad for the opportunity, in any case. 'You want to look?'

'Might's well see how they come through that soakin',' the other man agreed. Moncure climbed down, picking up the claw hammer and chisel, tendering them. 'Look for yourself. There's hoes in there,' he added

79

with a slight grin, as the trader reached for the nearest box; 'cultivatin' stuff in the others.'

The trader nodded, shoving the box back and choosing the next, as Moncure had intended. Apparently he had no ear for the subtleties of the language. His eyes gleamed as the board was pried back. The rifles were ready at hand. Hastily, almost nervously, he replaced the cover.

'Looks like what we've been waitin' for,' he agreed. Clearly, he was in no hurry to start the actual trading. Should anyone be watching from a distance, it was still light enough to see.

'You look hungry,' he added. 'My old woman's inside there. She'll give you something to eat.'

'I could use it,' Moncure agreed, accepting the invitation. The squaw who tended a stew, simmering in a pot, was young rather than old, and reasonably comely. Conversant with the preferences of white men, she dished some of the stew onto a tin plate, even providing a spoon. She watched anxiously as he tasted; then, as he appeared satisfied, she disappeared.

Squatting on his heels, Moncure ate hungrily, surveying the interior of the tepee by the flickering light reflected from something half concealed among the furs. It was a flask; the amber liquid had the appearance of tea.

As he ate, sounds informed him that his team was being unhitched and cared for. Moncure was tense, alert for the first sign of suspicion or alarm. Trading might begin at any time, or Gervais' man might decide to have a better look at the guns. To linger there long would mean disaster, yet any precipitate movement would arouse instant suspicion.

It was getting dark outside, and he dared wait no longer. He slipped under the side of the tepee, paused a moment, then rose to his full height. Voices from the vicinity of the wagon indicated that trading would not be long delayed. Firewood was being stacked in a big pile, so that the blaze would provide light.

The saddled horse was still tied to a sapling. Once mounted and off in the night, he'd be safe.

Moncure had it untied and was pulling himself into the saddle when he saw the Indian.

Probably chance rather than intent had brought the man wandering that way at so untimely a moment. He stopped, staring at the figure which loomed suddenly on the horse, sensing that something was not as it should be. He was not sufficiently alarmed to shout a warning; merely in a mood to investigate, a task which he clearly felt capable of performing.

Moncure moved fast and silently. He was off the horse on the far side, ducking under it and coming up, before either the cayuse or the Indian realized what was happening. As he came upright, he struck with his revolver, a short chopping blow to the side of the head.

The intruder slumped to the ground without a sound. Moncure's impulse was to jump back into the saddle and make a quick get-away. But if the man soon revived, an alarm would follow.

The tepee was still empty as Moncure ducked back inside. As he snatched the flask, he noticed another and larger pair of bottles. These, of dark glass, would hold a quart apiece.

The flask was of course the private property of the trader, undoubtedly containing a superior grade of liquor. The bottles would be filled with trade whiskey, to be given the Indians at the conclusion of the bartering.

As Moncure had anticipated, the stricken man was stirring, showing signs of reviving. Moncure lifted his head and held the neck of the flask to his lips. He swallowed, half choking. Another swallow went down more easily. Then, reviving, suddenly eager, he sat up, reaching for the flask with both hands. He was enjoying a long drink as Moncure rode silently away.

He would soon be too drunk either to

explain or remember, and his possession of the pilfered flask would speak for itself. That would provide a distraction, before anyone could think much about Moncure.

He was nodding in the saddle, and the smell of dawn was in the air, when the sentry at the gate challenged him. Sergeant Hauswitz, on duty, came forward, peering in amazement.

'What the—and is it yourself, Captain? Why, now, we hadn't expected you back so soon, sir. But it's happy I am to see you,' he added. 'You look a bit done in, if I may make so free.'

'I feel that way,' Moncure confessed. 'I think I'll turn in and get some sleep, for it's little enough acquaintance I've had with a blanket since I left. Will you be so good, Sergeant, as to inform the colonel, when he awakes, that everything went well, and that I will give him a detailed report when I awake?'

'I will do that, sir. And if I may again make so bold—then, sir, take your time and have a good sleep. I would say that you have earned it.'

It was a luxury to bathe and shave, with the sun of late afternoon slanting in through a window, then to eat hungrily before venturing forth. Normally Moncure would have frowned at such conduct, particularly on his own part, but now there were extenuating circumstances, not the least being the ball to

83

be held that evening. Being fresh for that ranked high on his list of priorities.

The word that he had returned would have circulated during the day. His lack of haste or concern would dispel any notion there was urgency in the situation, and that was desirable.

Myles Neilson viewed him with a faint smile as he entered and saluted.

'Take a chair, Captain. You look fresh as a summer snowflake, Dave—and ready to dance all night, I presume. There's nothing like a ball to lure a man back at the double, eh?'

'Well, I did keep the dance in mind, when circumstances permitted,' Moncure admitted. 'I am sorry that I kept you waiting for a report—'

The colonel waved a hand. 'Good Lord, Dave, I'm glad you slept. Hauswitz says you were so played out that you were staggering. He also informed me that everything went well. Considering where you must have been, that's almost incredible.'

'I had some luck along the way. I stumbled up to Gervais' cabin by Black Mountain as we'd planned, and apparently I was convincing. The tribes are gathering there already—quite a lot of them, as nearly as I could judge. My first break was that the agent's chief helper had a broken leg, leaving him short a teamster—to transport a wagonload of garden tools another day's journey distant.'

'So you hauled the tools?'

'Five dozen modern rifles, to be exact. Except that I delivered only a third of a dozen.'

'You mean that you managed to hide the others, and fool the Indians into accepting the shipment?'

'A heavy storm during the day afforded me cover for over an hour, and also washed away any sign. I believe the cache may go undiscovered until such time as we find it convenient to recover the guns, sir.'

Neilson eyed him in amazement.

'I wouldn't have believed it possible,' he admitted, 'for any one but you, at least. What about Hunk Gervais?'

'I have no doubt that by now he is afflicted with a case of jitters. There are questions to which he has no sure answer, and that will bother him. Perhaps not too much, however.' His tone took on an edge. 'He's the man I've been looking for most of this decade!'

Neilson stared. Familiar with Moncure's role during the war years, he understood, but the news was still astounding.

'What do you want to do?' he asked finally.

'For the moment—nothing. We know now what we suspected before—that big trouble is cooking, and who is stirring the brew. I would suppose that what has just happened may slow down any outbreak. Hunk and his Indians will probably sit back and wait, at least for a while, to see what may happen. My suggestion, sir, is that we allow them to reveal their uneasiness, meanwhile doing nothing to assuage their curiosity.'

'It sounds like an excellent procedure. In any case, we've plenty to keep us occupied for a while. I received further word today, regarding the place and procedure for the return of the captives. The exchange will take place near Black Mountain. Besides those you saw, other tribes are to gather there during the next few days.' He scowled. 'I don't like the sound of it, Dave. Gervais' territory—and if you're right about him, he must be directing, or at least be one of the chief planners.'

'I've not a doubt about that. But you have orders, I presume?'

'Since we at Lansing are closest, I'm in charge of procedures for the Army and the government—along with Mr. Gervais! It leaves us darned little room for maneuver.'

'Little enough,' Moncure granted, 'though we may have an ace or so in the hole.'

'We'll need all we can get. We are supposed to set out for the rendezvous day after tomorrow. We'll be sitting on a powder keg. As usual, in the case of something which concerns us so vitally, we're among the last to know what's going on. The report has been rather widespread, and of course has attracted wide attention, particularly among people with lost relatives. Some of the first of that group showed up here today. There will be more, wanting to go along with us.'

Moncure understood his apprehensions. What had happened could have had no effect on the negotiations, already under way for so long.

'It will be interesting, especially when I show up and Gervais recognizes me as a soldier. He'll likely guess what happened then.'

'It's a ticklish situation, on both sides. As for this return of captives—you should be pleased, Dave. You have a lot at stake.'

'I'm not hopeful,' Moncure said briefly.

Neilson did not pursue that tack. 'Do you think that they'll go through with that part in good faith?'

'Yes—until they are ready to strike. I doubt that there's an iota of good faith anywhere in this. It's a cover-up for all-out war, as soon as they deem the time right. They are trying to throw us off our guard until then, and the returned captives will be among us, to hit us from behind.'

'You've no faith in the loyalty of whites to their own blood, once they are returned?'

'Providing they have been captives no longer than half a year—yes. Those can still remember, and still hate an Indian. But if

87

they've been held for longer periods—I was about to say none at all. Let's make that scarcely any, sir. The Indian way with a captive is insidious, compounded of many things, some of which we find hard to understand. There is brutality, also kindness—a washing out of white blood, a pride in becoming Indian. Also, and this is important, there is a sense of shame and inferiority, after the humiliations they have been subjected to. Few can ever forget or hold up their heads among their own kind—especially the women.

'Men have different compensations. They can become warriors—and a white Indian is apt to be twice as fanatical as a real one! They learn to hate all over again—to hate all whites with an imperishable hatred! No. I honestly can't say that, even if it was all on an honest basis, I have very high hopes for any of this.'

Neilson's face was grim. Moncure's opinion ran parallel with his own, but the Army had not been consulted. It was merely up to them to do the work, to endeavour to keep the peace and see that security was not breached, while a such highly explosive situation developed.

'At least we can forget such matters for a few hours.' He shrugged. 'My niece was pleased and excited when she learned that you had managed to get back in time after all, Dave. You should have a pleasant evening.'

CHAPTER EIGHT

'I never expected to dance with a miracle man,' Serena observed, looking up at Moncure as they followed the music around the room. 'Yet I am assured by several of your fellow officers that you are no less.'

'They mistake the case entirely,' Moncure assured her. 'Every now and then I have a bit of luck—as at this moment. As to my last trip, I was pacing myself to return in time for this dance with you.'

'That, sir, is the finest compliment I have ever been paid.'

The look in her eyes, as well as the words, left him momentarily disconcerted. 'I'm sure that you've garnered plenty of compliments wherever you have gone.'

'I have received my share,' she agreed, 'which makes what you say the more outstanding.'

Finding him silent, she broached a fresh subject.

'Uncle Myles has agreed that the women of the fort may go along to watch the proceedings as the captives are returned. He was a bit undecided about allowing us, until I pointed out that our presence would be an indication of good faith on our side.'

'Were he not your uncle and my

commanding officer, I'd be inclined to say harsh things about him,' Moncure growled, and she saw that he was angry. 'You've prevailed against his better judgment, and I hope that we do not live to regret it.'

She eyed him in surprise, noting the turn of his phrase. 'But the Army is sufficient protection, surely, no matter what?'

'Protection? When we'll be outnumbered at least ten to one? I have no faith in *their* good faith.'

Serena surprised him by her next comment.

'If you really think it wise, I'll withdraw our request to go along—and I'm sure the others will agree.'

He hesitated, touched as much by her confidence as by the show of willingness to do whatever was best. His head-shake was uncertain.

'Now you place me on the horns of a dilemma,' he confessed. 'Speaking personally, I'd be delighted to have you ladies along. I would be more pleased to know that you were in a safe place. As it is—'

'What?' she prompted.

'I'm not sure. The fort could turn out to be a lure, also a trap, with you women here, and scarcely any men left to garrison it, the rest of us a day's ride distant. Perhaps the colonel had that in mind.'

'Do you really expect treachery and a

possible attack?'

'When one smells a skunk, it is safe to assume that one is on the prowl. Here the odor is too strong to miss.'

'But why?' she persisted. 'This sounds like a wonderful idea, on the part of both sides. The Indians will be making more than a token gesture of peace, by returning captives over whom innumerable tears must have been shed. What can be finer for the bereaved families?'

'On the face of it, it appears a dream come true,' he acknowledged. 'But have you ever watched a colorful insect drift across a placid pool? On the surface, all is serene—until suddenly a voracious trout gulps down the unlucky bug!'

'You paint a distressing picture of the pretty insect.'

'It's possible that it has feelings and a sense of fear, also a love of life, even as we. I keep wondering just where this idea emanated, whose notion it was. What I do know is not reassuring. And one thing I realize, which most may not. Many tribes will be gathering, some coming from long distances. In the past they have been unfriendly, usually hostile, groups who shun each other as they would a plague. Now they will be met on common ground, under a flag of truce, one real if not actually visible. Their hatred, if not turned against each other, will seek an outlet against

91

the people who are forcing them to give up captives who would prefer to remain among them!'

'You mean that you expect an attack?'

'Any concentration of warriors is risky, and now it's murderously so. The business of the Army has always been to see to it that no such gatherings took place, or, if they did, to keep them small and brief. This one has been arranged, forced upon us, and will be a huge gathering that may last for weeks. And every captive who is lost to them will fan the fires of their hate.'

★   ★   ★

He was shaving when Karl Hochhalter sought him out. Despite the long hours on the trail, then spending half the night dancing, Moncure looked fresh. The physician grunted.

'A pretty woman is like a tonic,' he observed. 'This morning most of the men look like the morning after, but not you. Nor do they regard you with unmixed enthusiasm. That you should make it back in time to steal half the dances from the belle of the ball—'

'What is troubling you, Karl? Certainly not my return.'

'It is sharp eyes and a sharper wit you have,' Hochhalter admitted. 'Not a word of this have I breathed to any other, but you were with me on that ride, when we found Old Bear dying. I returned to bury him and burn the tepee—and that part I accomplished. Only someone had been there ahead of me.'

'Ahead?' Moncure frowned. 'I should think that anyone would avoid the spot like a plague.'

'I had supposed so, also. But some ride in ignorance of the death which lies in wait—though any man with an eye in his head should have read the sign and understood. The part which worries me is that it may have been done through ignorance—or perhaps the opposite. In either case, the lid of hell may not be nailed so tightly shut as we had hoped.'

He sighed, turning to depart. At the doorway he delivered his real news.

'The blanket was gone—the gaudy thing in which Old Bear had wrapped himself, a potential pest rag. Where it may be now—or who may be encasing himself in it, loving the colors and with small scruple that he appropriated what the old chief was past needing ever again—well, we may have an answer when least we relish it!'

It was a considerable and somewhat motley cavalcade that wound out from the fort and toward the north. It consisted of cavalry and foot soldiers, supply wagons and women, along with a scattering of other vehicles and civilians as gaudy as the first colors of fall. Many seemed to feel that they were going on a holiday rather than on business; there was almost a carnival air of expectancy. Well, let them rejoice while they could.

Their going left the fort too thinly held for comfort. But they had to make a bold display, to show themselves unafraid before watchful foes. It was the old game of never having enough with which to control too much, a handful of men delegated to police a continent. Only this time the stakes were higher than usual, and the game a new one, being played by new rules not of their choosing.

They would take two days to cover the miles to Black Mountain, chiefly because of the dozens of people who had streamed into the fort. Some had arrived with an escort from Starke, but others were making it on their own, apparently convinced that there was nothing more to be feared from Indians who had suddenly turned tractable.

These were families or representatives of families who had lost relatives. With some the thing was recent and the wounds still fresh, and with others most of a lifetime had passed since the tragedy. Now that there was hope and promise they had turned wildly eager, feeling that they could not wait even an additional month or day for the Army to return the lost ones; they were determined to be on hand, hoping to be speedily reunited with loved ones long lost.

It was difficult to stop them from going along, impossible to make them understand the situation or restrain their hopes. The best that could be done was to provide an escort and keep them under reasonable control. They were one more of the problems.

A perfect example was to be found in Miss Samantha DeLoss. Somehow she had learned what was toward in time to come all the way from Massachusetts, enduring the hardships of the road to be on hand when her sister Teresa should be reunited with her.

Thirty years before they had been twins, crossing the plains with their parents. Teresa had been captured, and never recovered. Hope had flamed high a dozen times, only to burn low again. All of those years, clinging to the conviction that one day all would be made right, Miss Samantha had lived in the ancestral home to which the family had returned.

'It was a mistake for a family such as ours ever to venture into so raw a land,' she confided. 'Papa realized it, but alas, too late, where poor Teresa was concerned. Still, I find much comfort in the old saying: All's well that ends well.'

She was convinced that this time her loved sister would be restored to her. Happily she confided to Serena the details of the homecoming reception which was being planned for Arlington when they should return. All the relatives and neighbors were uniting to insure that it would be a gala affair.

Moncure, listening at the edge of the firelight, felt constrained to dampen her high hopes, so that the ultimate shock might not be unbearable.

'I wouldn't set my hopes too high, Miss DeLoss,' he observed, 'even should everything go well in the proceedings. You—if you will pardon a personal reference—are still a young and charming woman. But have you stopped to think that your sister may have aged?'

'She is my twin, therefore my exact age,' Miss DeLoss pointed out. 'So why should there be any difference?'

'You have been raised, so to speak, in the bosom of your family, among friends, and in conditions as nearly ideal as possible. But during that time, your sister has been a captive in a wilderness, among half-savage people. There is bound to be a difference.'

'Quite possibly,' Miss Samantha acknowledged, dabbing at her eyes with a wisp of handkerchief. 'But she is a DeLoss, and pride of family runs strong in us. Besides, love will overcome all obstacles. We were very close my sister and I.'

Moncure stared helplessly after the woman as she stalked away to the tent she shared with another lady. Serena ventured a word.

'Perhaps it won't be too much of a change—'

'Her sister, if she is alive, will be an old woman—a squaw. She will be the mother of Indians, with no remembrance of any other life. She will have forgotten all the English which once she knew. I doubt if she will even remember having had a sister, and if so, she will not care.'

Serena stared at him in horror, before she turned soberly to her own tent, with a better understanding of what lay ahead. In all this, she remembered, Moncure was worse off than most. He had both a brother and a sweetheart among the lost, and there was a chance that one or both of them might turn up within the next few days.

They had been in sight of Black Mountain through most of the day, and gradually it was growing in size, taking on shape and detail, like a mirage becoming reality. Moncure could see the cabin where he had spent a night as Hunk Gervais' guest. Now, as Indian agent an important figure in what was due to take place, Gervais came riding to meet them, mounted on a white horse, resembling an overstuffed doll in the saddle. Today he was carefully attired and shaven and accompanied by an aide. If recent events had shaken him, he had recovered from his apprehension and chosen to carry on.

Moncure watched with amusement as Gervais' attention went automatically to the colonel, then shifted to focus suddenly on himself. The usual rich color of whiskey and good living fled above the golden-bearded cheeks. Gervais goggled, recognition and dismay struggling in his face. Whatever he had feared as a result of the debacle of the rifles, this was worse than even his lively imagination had pictured. This man wore a captain's uniform.

Moncure gave no sign, and a flicker of doubt replaced the consternation in the agent's eyes. Could it be possible that he was mistaken, that there might be two men so similar in appearance? The disappearance of the other man, coupled with the loss of the guns, argued against that.

He mumbled an uncertain word of greeting, and Neilson, hiding a smile, introduced them.

'This is Captain Moncure, Mr. Gervais. My second in command.'

Moncure extended a hand, pulling off his glove.

'Glad to meet you, Mr. Gervais,' he agreed cordially.

Gervais accepted the handshake, half expecting the clasp to tighten while words of arrest were pronounced. Here, in the flesh, was his old nemesis, and it seemed inconceivable that Moncure could fail to know him from the past, however well he had covered his trail.

Yet if Moncure was sure, would he fail to act? On the other hand, he might be playing a cautious game, aware of the power which the agent could call upon, the inherent risks should the Indians be offended. Gervais was highly popular with his charges, the Cheyennes.

It would do no harm to let him stew awhile, Moncure reasoned. He was mildly pleased at the lack of disturbance evident here at the center of intrigue. The encampments of several different tribes could be seen in the distance, above the canyon, but all was calm. Had any approach to the platforms in the sky been discovered, along with the desecration of the graves, the tribes would have been boiling like a kicked-in ant hill. So it followed that his cache was relatively safe.

Here were all the elements for an explosion, but no one on either side was quite ready to set it off.

Camp was pitched where a pleasant strip of pine trees and a scattering of spruce offered shade. Ample water from a cluster of springs sprang as rivulets, joining to form a stream that hurried toward the river. Ahead lay a business which could not be hurried, much as some might desire to; there would be endless ceremony and palaver, and weeks might pass before anything was accomplished.

Meanwhile the supply wagons, winding up from Starke, were getting through with less trouble than had been the case this past twelvemonth. Outwardly that was one more good sign, but Moncure was suspicious of all friendly gestures.

One day soon his curiosity would be satisfied, and he would learn whose intelligence was back of all this planning and plotting. Apparently it had to be Hunk Gervais, for only the agent was situated so he could pull the diverse tribes together, at the same time profiting by being the catalytic agent in mass destruction. It had to be someone with all the qualities of position, leadership and authority, for lesser men would founder on the twin rocks of suspicion and jealousy.

Yet somehow he doubted that Gervais could be the one. Gervais, or Oldhouse, was clever, and he had been proved unscrupulous, but here was plotting which seemed far beyond him. During the war, as one of the ring, he had been an effective agent, but not the brains behind the renegade enterprise.

The sooner that riddle was resolved, the slighter became the risk of hearing war whoops at dawn.

There were complaints about the military discipline imposed upon the camp, affecting everyone who had made the journey. Some had anticipated that they could rush headlong across to the tribal encampments and, finding relatives awaiting them with the same eagerness, be instantly reunited. Colonel Neilson made it plain that he was running the show.

The Indian encampments were a mile or so beyond, most of them pitched along the rim of the canyon, others down inside it, near the river. There were villages of Cheyenne, of Crow and Pawnee and Kansa visible from the headquarters tent; still others were out of sight, each separate from the others, yet in curious and unusual proximity. Frowning, Neilson stroked his boot with the lash of a riding whip.

'That I should live to see this day, to see the lion and the lamb lying down together! Truly it is a day of miracles—if we can believe our eyes. Which I don't!'

'Prestidigitators have a saying that the hand is quicker than the eye.' Moncure shrugged. 'This will be proof of that.'

Though he gave no outward sign, he noted where Serena Sullivan strolled in the cool of the evening, with Lieutenant Atkinson, who was clearly bemused by such company. With a light word, she left him and crossed to where Moncure stared somberly at the softly glowing eyes ranged along the rim of darkness, the waning cook fires of a hundred lodges.

'You look glum, David,' she observed.

'As glum as young Mr. Atkinson feels at this moment,' Moncure agreed. 'He is reflecting unhappily on the fickleness of woman—even such a woman as yourself, Serena. As for me—you have lifted my spirits as his wane. But even from this distance, it's plain that the chiefs are gathering, smoking the pipe and exchanging observations.'

'Is that bad? Isn't it an indication of better feeling than usual between the tribes?'

'That's what I'm afraid of,' he confessed gloomily. 'Who has persuaded them to show such civility, even at a gathering such as this? Will you grant me pardon if I seem to disdain your company—even use you as an instrument for another purpose?'

She caught her breath, then nodded, studying his face in the half-light. 'I will be glad to help in any way I can.'

'Good girl. It's a shame to waste such an evening, such company—' He sighed and beckoned to Atkinson, then, at his approach, spoke softly.

'Lieutenant, Miss Sullivan and I are going to stroll for a quarter of a mile or so toward those distant lights. Then I propose to keep on, alone, to do a bit of looking about. But should any chance to be observing us, it should look as though we had turned back together. Can you contrive to be there to escort her on the return, without any change being notice-able even to reasonably sharp eyes?'

Atkinson looked startled. Then he nodded. 'I'll manage it, sir. It should not be too difficult.'

Moncure offered his arm. 'Shall we stroll?' he asked.

He could feel Serena's excitement in the quiver of her arm, linked with his own, but her voice was steady, her laugh soft and warm in the dusk. He felt the same sort of excitement, not all of it because of what might lie ahead.

Ostensibly there was peace hereabouts. Somewhere, probably back at more distant camps, the captives would be held, awaiting the parleys. Even so, for an alien white, a man in uniform, to be discovered prowling in the vicinity of the lodges, particularly the lodges where the chiefs were gathered—

He did not intend to be discovered, but there were always risks. In this camp he had noticed another oddity. There were no dogs, which might bark or growl betrayingly. The dogs had been left at some other more permanent camp, which probably was located not too many miles back in the hills. This gave rise to another interesting speculation.

It was mostly a matter of patience and caution, watching, picking a careful course, guided by knowledge and what he had been able to see, making use of his ears. The lodge was remote, hidden, and large—

unquestionably a chief's. The flaps were tied back, since the evening was warm. From where Moncure crouched in a clump of brush, he could see inside at least a score of head men, leaders from all the tribes. They squatted in a circle, taking an occasional puff of the pipe, listening while others took turns speaking. Some, judging from the shadows they cast, were using sign language, due to the disparity of tongues. Again, voices rolled sonorously in the hush of night.

He edged closer to obtain a glimpse of the speaker. It was a man who used the Cheyenne fluently, and that was a tongue which Moncure understood. He stared, amazement changing to disbelief, and gained a knowledge laced with bitterness.

Somehow the impossible had a way of happening, and always at the worst possible times. The man was a Cheyenne and a chief. Yet in spite of the passage of years and the disparity of their lives and customs, Moncure knew that at last he looked upon his own brother.

CHAPTER NINE

When at length he allowed himself to relax within his cabin, Gervais was panting and sweating. Outwardly he had remained smiling, thankful for the golden brush of beard which helped hide his thoughts, but liking matters less and less as he pondered them. That Leafelt should be Moncure was upsetting enough, but that Moncure should be Dunstan—

Somehow he had never associated the names, and putting together all that he knew left him on the verge of panic. Imagined dangers were suddenly real, and ten times worse than he had supposed.

He delved among the pile of skins, buffalo robes piled six deep, and brought to light a flask. Not until he had drunk deep did he begin to relax, sinking onto the robes, staring at the vacant bunks on the opposite wall. It had been enough of an ordeal, wondering if the officers were playing with him—

Undoubtedly they were, and he was in deadly peril. He was the Indian agent and, as such, answerable to Washington rather than the Army. But they might take matters into their own hands, especially if they suspected what was in the wind. With Dunstan there, that was a very real danger.

There would be ample justification for such a course, since treason was a hanging offense, and even without his past record, which was known to Moncure, gun-running rated almost as treason. Should the colonel decide to take up his case, with evidence to back his action, as military commander he might hang Gervais out of hand. Such extreme action would be risky, but in balancing the hazard against the dangers should he fail to act, Neilson was just the man who might decide to take drastic measures. Yet who could ever have supposed that the down-at-the-heels wanderer in search of succor would turn out to be an Army man?

The whiskey had its effect, and Gervais was able to think more calmly. Whatever they might suspect or even know, they were not taking immediate or risky action, and that argued that perhaps they might not be too sure. Or it could be that they dared not risk angering the Indians at this juncture. The palavers and the exchange were at hand, and in that he was supposed to play a key part. Moreover, he was popular with his dark-skinned charges.

There was reason for such popularity, and if it came to a showdown, what had he to fear? He had but to say the word, to give the permission they were ardently seeking, and the Indians would back him to the last man, a full thousand warriors. Against them, the Army—always inadequate in numbers, and now more so than ever—would be helpless. They would be massacred, killed to the last man, and it could be accomplished in a matter of hours.

Perhaps it would be well to give the word now, to order a strike before dawn, while they were off guard, not expecting anything so grim. The eager braves would spring to action at his word. For they beheld a dream in the process of fulfilment. For the first time in many a weary decade, the fighting men were united in purpose against a common enemy. Ancient tribal animosities had been submerged, half by oratory and persuasion, half by the realization of the larger struggle for existence which had to be waged as a people rather than as peoples.

That had been a vision, the dream of a few far-sighted leaders, almost since the coming of the first white settlers along the Atlantic; the dream of uniting the tribes and destroying the light-skinned invaders, to the last man.

Several times over the years the dream had all but come to fruition, and a few times there had actually been bloody massacre, but on a limited scale. Always, fears and hatreds had conspired to prevent a united effort. With each failure it had become clearer to the leaders that they had to succeed or face destruction. Soon the white men would be too strong for them, the last chance forever gone.

Gervais smiled cynically. If the fools did but know it, it was already too late, a century too late. By a concerted uprising they might wipe out the garrisons at Lansing and at Starke, perhaps at another post or so, and sweep the prairie clean. For a brief summer they could rejoice and ride tall, but the summer was short and winter came swift and cold, as it would for these children of nature in their vainglory.

But by that time he would have reached California with the fruits of his treachery; going under another identity, after presumably being killed along with all the other whites in the general carnage. That was an important part of his plan, for at any time now some prying clerk in a musty office might discover the discrepancies in his record, then do a bit of tracing.

Once such a search started, it would not take long to find out that the real Hunk Gervais was ten years in his grave; or that the man who masqueraded under that identity had been sentenced to be shot for high treason nearly that long ago. And the sentence still stood.

He'd worked things surprisingly well, as one of the ring, the net of intrigue and deception. Now, however, it was becoming worn, with too many tears in it, and this was the only way out. Once officially dead, far gone from his old haunts, there would be nothing more to fear.

Starting again, he'd lead a life of sober respectability.

He had found eager allies among his charges, intelligent men with whom to work. But the hour was not quite ripe. The loss of half a hundred guns in the past few days, guns of which no trace had been found despite desperate searching, left a dangerous gap. Those rifles might still be found, and others were on the way. Chief Little Wolf had agreed with him that the time was not yet.

Little Wolf had also been dangerously angry, scathingly sarcastic. Yet how could he have done otherwise? There had been no one else to send with that wagonload of guns, no one whom he could really trust. It had not appeared a risk at all. The wagon and its driver would be watched all the way, and there was no possible hiding place—

The combination of the storm and Moncure had been his undoing. Yet it still seemed incredible.

Gervais took another pull at the bottle. For all the darkness of the situation, still he had nothing to fear. He could call down destruction upon his enemies, if necessary, whenever he chose. None who knew his record could doubt that he would.

The error, in the end, might turn out to be the mistake of those men in blue who counted themselves so clever. Gervais slipped out into the settling night.

He found a ready messenger, sent word ahead, and went part way himself, both to show a willing spirit and to save time. He waited near the rim of the canyon, its mighty abyss a pool of night, and presently Little Wolf materialised out of the gloom.

'You sent for me?' he asked.

This, too, was better. The Cheyenne chief could speak the tongue of his fathers as fluently as did Gervais, but normally he refused to use or even acknowledge an understanding of English. Here, with the two of them alone, he dispensed with meaningless ceremonies.

'I had to talk with you,' Gervais explained. 'I think I know what happened to the rifles.'

'What?' Little Wolf was never a man to waste time on matters which were vital, and the vanished guns were a sore spot.

'I believe that the Army knows where they are. It turns out that I made a mistake. The man I hired to drive the team, who disappeared in the night after delivering the wagon, is an Army man. His name is Moncure—Captain David Moncure.'

He smiled to himself in the half-light, sensing how the other man stiffened. It had taken considerable probing to discover the history and background of this formidable chief of the Cheyennes, but here and there he had picked up a word or a clue. Though there were many war chiefs among the Cheyennes, none was more feared than Little Wolf, or held a more enduring hatred for the whites. Yet he himself was a white man, whose name had once been Moncure.

Little Wolf hotly rejected the accusation that he was white now in any sense whatever, and he disdained the name of Moncure. He had been only a boy when taken captive, and for a time he had remained intractable. Adopted as the son of a chieftain, an all but inevitable change had taken place. He was completely certain that all vestiges of white blood had been washed from his veins in various ceremonies before he reached warrior's estate. To look at him, one would suppose him fully Indian, though a closer study was revealing.

Some things could not be altered. A shaven head, except for the scalp lock, war paint (now washed off as a matter of temporary expediency), other manners and customs made a difference. The deep burn of sun and winter wind had rendered his skin nearly as dark as that of any fullblood, and even his eyes seemed darker, more filled with hate.

Still the profile of nose and jaw, the look of a face, remained. Having seen David Moncure at closer range, Gervais could readily trace a family resemblance.

It was strange how, when a white man became an Indian and was taught to hate, his venom toward his own people became so much worse even than an Indian's. Yet it was so. But the toughest armor always retained some chinks, certain points of vulnerability. Priding himself on a certain detached philosophy, Gervais found this an interesting study.

Moncure, of late, had become a feared and

famous name along the border. Little Wolf was a name equally well-known, at which strong men blanched. The scalps he had taken and the feats he had committed were the envy of his fellow chiefs.

'Moncure?' Little Wolf repeated. His calmness was an indication of his mood. '*He* stole those rifles?'

'He drove the wagon.'

Little Wolf fingered the knife at his belt. For this visit, he had laid aside war axe and scalp lock, but he insisted on keeping the bowie.

'He can be made to tell where.'

'It wouldn't do, Little Wolf. Not right now. I fear his tongue would prove stubborn. After all, he's a lot like you—being your brother.'

Little Wolf's voice was cold. 'I have no brother.'

'Suit yourself about that. But you're a warrior, and so is he. He has a reputation as a fighter, and you'll have to admit that he has the courage to take risks.'

'No matter. I can deal with him.'

'Later, perhaps. Now now. It could spoil everything. We are not quite ready.'

The Indian was silent for a moment. Then he nodded.

'I can wait. It will even be interesting to play a game. But why did you send for me?'

'I think he's playing a cat and mouse game

with me—or *he* thinks he is. Two can play such a game. I just wanted you to understand, to be ready, in case something comes up.'

Listening carefully to the harangue, Moncure was conscious of a variety of emotions, some of which he had supposed were too deeply buried to be revived. He had doubted his lost brother would show up for this business of returning captives, whatever the terms of the treaty, and if indeed he was still alive. Yet here he was, beyond much possibility of mistake. Though an Indian and a Cheyenne of fearsome reputation, Little Wolf was undeniably a Moncure.

At least he had been born a Moncure. Listening to him in the softness of the summer night, Moncure had no illusion that he would ever again be one, or even give lip service to being a white man.

Here were the answers to questions which had puzzled him, the brains and leadership behind the plot, a capacity which Hunk Gervais did not possess. This man was a natural leader, far-sighted, careful in planning. His words, the unmistakable hold which he exerted over chieftains of rival tribes, made that clear.

That at least a part of his ability to see so clearly and plan beyond the moment or the hour might be the heritage of his white blood, Little Wolf would have denied vehemently.

Here, however, was the real leader, the force behind the conspiracy.

That a conspiracy such as Moncure had envisioned was afoot was made clear as Little Wolf talked. The various tribes were gathered here, ostensibly in friendship with the white man, to fulfill a new agreement and return all captives whose blood had once been white, and who had been taken over the years. Moncure took note of the phrasing, 'whose blood had once been white.'

Little Wolf was well aware of the dismay and heart-break which even the consideration of such a course engendered among his own people, meaning the loss of sons or brothers, wives or mothers. However, they should not be dismayed. If they carried out the terms of the agreement, the white men's suspicions would be allayed and any lingering fears removed.

When the moment came, before the camp should be struck, the red men, to whom the land belonged, would taste vengeance for all the wrongs done to them by the whites, both past and present. He promised that it should be more than a taste; they would drink deep of white blood. Not one white would be left alive, save those who might make good captives.

There would be no reason for anyone to grieve when companions, captives for long years, were given up and handed over. It

114

would be for a short time only, for all of them would be returned.

The captives themselves, who were temporarily to be restored, would play an important role, rendering themselves highly useful, showing themselves true Indians. By submitting docilely to this thing, pretending that they were willing to return to white ways, they would be in a perfect position to kill many whites when the hour struck.

Little Wolf finished amid grunts of approval. No one else bothered to speak formally. There was nothing more to be said. He dominated the gathering, and no one questioned his plan or his authority.

The gathering broke up, the chiefs drifting away to their own camps, their own lodges. Moncure took note of another incongruous note. Normally, when Indians made ready for war, especially on a large scale, there was much preparation, dancing and making medicine. Perhaps that had been done already, but here normal procedures were repressed, a façade of friendship presented to the men who were to be duped.

Not until the last one had departed did Moncure make his own way back. He had found out what he wanted to know, but there was nothing about it to diminish the depression which had settled upon him. The peril which threatened every white within a radius of hundreds of miles was bad enough.

That the implacable leader of the red men should be white, a Moncure and his own brother, was far worse.

CHAPTER TEN

The camps had grown silent when Moncure made his way back, and even the challenge of the sentry at his approach was soft-voiced. Orders had been given that there should be nothing which might cause alarm, unless an emergency arose. Moncure took care that his tall figure and uniform should be outlined in the light of the moon.

A light still burned in the commandant's tent, and he was admitted at once. To his surprise, Serena was there. She arose from a camp chair at his entrance; then her eyes widened as she studied him.

'What is it, Captain?' she breathed. 'You're as white as we're made to feel, by contrast with these people—' Color stained her cheeks, and she turned quickly to her uncle. 'I'm sorry. I didn't mean to interfere. I'll go at once.'

'I'd like to have you stay, if you don't mind,' Moncure returned wearily. 'What I have to report concerns you, too, in a way.' At Neilson's sign, he sank into another chair. 'I saw my brother.'

116

The quick interest in their faces denoted their understanding. That the lost lad might turn up here, after all these years, had seemed a remote possibility. Still, in business such as this, the unusual was almost commonplace.

'You ventured into their territory, alone?' Neilson countered. It was half a reproof, half a question.

'We're supposed to be enjoying a friendly truce.' Moncure's shrug was mocking. 'I crouched in the brush and listened as the head men of most of the tribes discussed what *their* program should be.'

Neilson offered no criticism. Serena had mentioned the ruse employed by Moncure. Such conduct bordered on rashness, but boldness was called for in a desperate game. None of this had been of Neilson's planning or with his approval; others, mostly men in distant and safe places, had indulged their fancies and made the rules, without even extending the courtesy of consulting him. That the idea had been carefully planted in their minds would have surprised them. Finally they had issued orders which he was supposed to carry out. They had disregarded the hazards, convinced that those had been removed.

There was nothing new in such a course; theorists were always rushing in where practical men hesitated. Government bureaus who looked upon the Indian as a

117

misunderstood child, truants who misbehaved only because they were not properly approached, had a way of going over the heads of the Army. The men in blue were supposed to carry out instructions, but were relegated to the doubtful status of errand boys. It was one more of the pile of dryly bitter bones which a man in uniform was forced to accept.

'Your brother was a member of that council?' Neilson asked.

'He dominated it. I recognized him beyond any doubt. If I was to shave my head, stain my face with berry juice and change to Cheyenne dress, I could almost pass for him; and in this uniform he could fool half the enlisted men. His voice was characteristic. Except that he spoke Cheyenne, it could have been my father speaking. Father was ten years old when he arrived in this country, but he never outgrew the Welsh accent. That must be more than a matter of environment, something in the blood and fibre. Even hearing those tones in Cheyenne, it took me back a score of years.'

'You are telling us that *he* is the man who had the plan for a united Indian confederacy?'

'He has the dream, the vision. A white man with an Indian heart. From their point of view, it amounts to a magnificent conception.'

'And with no disrespect for the ability of many of these red friends of ours, it would

118

take a white man to come up with such a plan,' Neilson agreed thoughtfully. 'His is a broader view, while they are unconsciously handicapped by ages of tribal history and tradition.'

'That may be it,' Moncure agreed. 'Anyhow, it's clear that he's sold them on the idea. They are going along with this matter of returning captives, to convince us of their peaceful intentions, so that they can take us off guard and wipe us out to the last man. The repatriated captives will be instructed to stick knives in our backs at the proper time.'

Serena listened in horrified fascination. These two, her uncle and this other man, who had come to be rather special in a matter of days, had guessed what was in the wind, envisioning the plan with terrible accuracy. Confirmation was both helpful and startling. That the driving force behind the plan should turn out to be Moncure's brother made it worse.

'You haven't told us his name,' Neilson reminded Moncure.

'Chief Little Wolf.'

Prepared as he was, Neilson recoiled. A white man might consider the name unfitting, thinking that at least it should be Wolf Who Kills. It marked another difference in custom and thinking that both the Cheyennes and the man who bore it were satisfied with the name. Little Wolf had come to be the epitome of

119

savage cruelty to a dozen restless tribes.

'So they will wait until all the captives have been returned? It's a good plan.'

'Too good,' Moncure agreed. 'Should you ask for help from Fort Starke, any who march out from there will be cut off before they can reach us. We're where they want us, well away from the walls of the fort, with no chance of receiving any help.'

'And odds of ten to one!' Neilson looked thoughtfully at Serena. 'I should have never allowed you—or any of the women—to come along. Yet with only a handful as garrison at the fort, it's no safer. And now you're here . . . I suppose there is no chance that you could appeal to your brother, after a few days in which to become acquainted?'

Moncure's head-shake was weary.

'It would be wasted breath. He's not a white renegade; they are generally bad enough. He's Indian—with the distasteful remembrance of the fact that his blood was white to begin with, which in his mind becomes a taint to be wiped out only by the spilling of more white blood.'

The summary, Neilson felt, was only too accurate. 'Have you any ideas, then?'

'Nothing very helpful, I'm afraid. Certain possibilities occur to me, but even to try to make use of them might precipitate the crisis. I guess we'll just have to watch for the breaks. After all, though they're united at the moment in common hatred against us, these tribes have warred with one another for centuries, and old scars remain. If they should start to quarreling among themselves—'

'That might or might not help.' Neilson tugged thoughtfully at an ear lobe. 'Also, we're supposed to exert a guardianship over them—however much they resent it—also to be concerned for their welfare.'

'I know, sir. Also, Little Wolf rules them with an iron hand.' He went on slowly, 'If something should happen to remove him—in such a way that the blame would attach to others, not us—'

He saw the shock in Serena's eyes as she bit her lip unbelievingly. He felt unutterably weary, for whatever Little Wolf might think or do, he was still Moncure's brother, and for a score of years Moncure had remembered him as a small boy, quick and eager, looking up to his older brother in adoration and trust.

But that was a dream, and this was reality. Given an initial success here, a victory to inspire his diverse warriors and unite a score of tribes behind his banner, forging them into an army instead of scores of small isolated bands, Little Wolf might win many more battles. His was the white way of thinking, as opposed to the red, and his record as a war leader unmistakably followed the pattern.

It was not that white men were braver or

better fighters; merely that the two traditions of warfare were utterly dissimilar. An Indian would hit and run, finding no disgrace in withdrawal, so that he might live to fight another day. It was largely a matter of the individual, as opposed to a united force obeying one leader. Little Wolf understood the difference and intended to correct it, adopting the methods of the men he hated, that in so doing he might rid the land of them.

If he succeeded in the first few fights, a vast number of people would die over a mighty expanse of wilderness. Sooner or later the force would be broken, against the settled lands, the cities, the discipline of the Army of the United States. But that might lie years in the future.

It would be a bold adventure, a glorious dream from the standpoint of the red man. Little Wolf's trouble was that it had come too late, and that, lacking the white man's education, he was like other red men, unable to envision the massive numbers against whom his pitifully few warriors would be pitted.

There was ruthlessness in Little Wolf, not only as a matter of policy but as a way of life. Ashamed of the taint of white blood, even though he believed that the last vestiges of it had been washed from his veins, he had whole-heartedly adopted the Indian outlook on life and war. Toward enemies you were ruthless, because that was war, and you fought to win.

There was a streak of ruthlessness in David Moncure also, since, trained as a soldier, he accepted the same premise. In war the purpose was to win. There was never anything chivalrous about murder.

Balanced in the scale were thousands, perhaps tens of thousands of lives, the majority of them those of women and children, of the innocent, the noncombatants. The red man made no distinction, and if he sought justification, it was readily to be found in similar brutal slaughters of squaws and children by whites, even those wearing the uniform, who too many times had run berserk.

In such a holocaust there could be no winners; only losers. Victory, like a flapping vulture, might perch first on one banner, then on the other, but its beak and claws would be rank with blood and carrion. Should there be no other way, then better to set the tribes quarreling again among themselves, destroying unity, but saving them from the folly of ultimate destruction.

They dispersed soberly, Moncure escorting Serena to her quarters, lingering a moment in the scented night. The great purple dome of ten million stars seemed to whisper of peace and serenity; this was the season of growing things, of earth approaching ripening and harvest. The distant river, plunging and foaming through the depths of the canyon in a series of cascades, echoed here in a murmurous lullaby. The spiciness of pine perfumed the night.

'I'm sorry, David,' Serena whispered. 'But I'm proud to know you! And, knowing you, I can understand how it is that your brother is such a leader!'

She was inside then, and he turned back to his own quarters, walking like a man bemused. These might well be the last days of life for any of them. Still, it was hard to think of death, and difficult not to dream, or to sort out dreams and keep reality in mind.

A sentry paced slowly, and he thought of cautioning him, even of doubling the guard, but to do so would tip their hand and reveal that they were suspicious. For the moment they must tread a razor-thin path, since that was the balance between life and death.

Under the brightness of the July sun there was the illusion of peace, as whites, particularly the families who had made the hopeful journey there, ventured to the edges of the Indian encampments. They were watched shyly but with no sign of hostility. Indians moved along the rim of the canyon, or came in turn to watch the whites. It was like a play on a giant stage, and only officers as experienced as Moncure observed that the numbers of red men in each camp were held to a careful minimum. Most of the force which he knew had gathered remained back in the hills, out of sight.

The preliminaries got under way almost on schedule, a meeting of representatives from both sides. They took puffs at the rank-tasting pipe as it was passed gravely about the circle. Neither Little Wolf nor any chiefs of importance participated.

The Indians listened to the reading of a paper, prepared a thousand miles away, stating what was expected of them and what they must do. There was a promise of favors in return, most of these nebulous and uncertain.

Faces which could smile or grimace as readily as any remained gravely impassive. There was a feast, at which Colonel Neilson and Hunk Gervais and others met with chiefs from all the tribes, and they ate in an outward spirit of good will. Moreover, if there was hypocrisy there, it was not one-sided.

There had been a time when the smoking of the peace pipe had been a grave, almost a sacred ceremony, but too many broken treaties had reduced it to an all but meaningless formality. Nor did Little Wolf participate in this, remaining discreetly out of sight.

The day was spent in necessary formalities, with dances and restrained entertainment to fill the evening. The Indians accepted, making it clear that they did so under pressure and not of their own acord. A chief of the Pawnees had dwelt on that aspect of the matter.

'It is true, as all know, that there are some among us who once were white,' he conceded. 'At one time they were what you now term them—captives. But in most cases that was a long time ago—as far removed as the dawn from the sunset, the spring from the fall.' His voice took on a note of deep earnestness.

'The taking of captives in war or battle is an ancient custom, one which, I am told, is honored as much among the white men as among the red. For it there are many reasons, but who shall deny that it is better to take captives than to slay?

'What the customs of the whites may be in regard to their captives I do not know. But we whose skin is burned darker by the sun are not unjust with those of other hues who dwell among us. It is true that some captives are put to death while war persists, and that again is a custom among the whites. Some captives become slaves, and again that has been a custom among the whites. How long has it been since the great war, before which those with black skins were considered slaves?'

He was silent a moment, then continued. 'In our case, most captives are adopted as sons or daughters, or they marry with us and become one with our people. If you will ask them fairly, openly, what are their desires, whether they prefer to return to a life largely forgotten, or to remain with husbands or wives, with sons and daughters, they will tell you that they are no longer white, but Indian; that among us they have found happiness, and that to tear them away, to a life become new and strange, is not what they want, but something they fear. If permitted to choose, they will remain with their families. To take them against their will is to make them captive; not to free them.'

It was an impassioned and sobering plea, and totally without effect. Not many were convinced, for this ran contrary to hopes and long-cherished beliefs, and it was inconceivable that any white could prefer hardship and filth to the blessings of civilization.

Even had they been convinced, willing to allow the choice to remain with the captives, their hands were tied. To those in far-distant places who had drawn up the terms, it had been even more inconceivable that such a situation might exist. It was provided that all white captives, whatever their age or sex, were to be returned. There were no exceptions, no provisions for change. Though he had not been consulted, Colonel Neilson, as commandant in charge of the operation, was required to see that the terms were carried out.

Beyond the voicing of the plea, there was no outward objection. There might be individual protests when the actual transfer got under way, but the red men, for reasons of their own, were outwardly submissive. No professional actors could have done better in their roles.

Optimism ran high among the relatives who had journeyed so far to this rendezvous. Some of them had glimpsed white men and women, even boys and girls, among the Indians. The captives were at hand, and soon they would be happily reunited. That danger might lurk close, with so many hostiles near at hand, they refused to believe. Here was proof of amity, and in any case, was not the Army on hand to protect them?

CHAPTER ELEVEN

The actual business of repatriation got under way the next day. Now that the necessary formalities had been observed, everyone was anxious to proceed. Though it was carefully masked, Moncure detected the same impatience among the Indians. An important part of the plan of attack lay in planting the captives among the whites, where, well instructed in their roles, they could strike from behind at a given signal. Though confident both of overwhelming numbers and the advantage of surprise, Little Wolf was too good a general to overlook such details.

At best, the return of the captives would be a time-consuming chore. Each case had to be dealt with individually, the identity of each captive established insofar as possible, and whether or not there was anyone to receive him. Some relatives were on hand and eager, but many captives would undoubtedly turn up whose families had either been wiped out or who had given up hope and forgotten them with the lapse of time.

Even had there been no grim overtones to the affair, Moncure would have been convinced that it was a bad business, which in most cases could lead only to disappointment. He would have agreed to the procedure on a voluntary basis—providing that captives who were willing to return should do so, while individual decisions should be made in borderline cases. Where families or friends were not on hand, and the captives were clearly Indian in thought and sympathy, eager to remain as they were, they should be given the choice.

Under the terms of the agreement, nothing of that sort was permissible. There were to be no exceptions.

As a military man, he would see that orders

were obeyed, so far as possible. That the whole amounted to little more than a mummers' parade was at once an aggravation and an opportunity. The certainty of bad faith on the one side gave room for discretion on their own.

The first captive who came, moving unwillingly, was a woman. Another squaw accompanied her, and at first glance there was little to choose between them. Both clutched blankets, staring with eyes which gave an impression of sightlessness. An interpreter explained.

She was white, or had been as a child. Of her early life she remembered only a little, having dwelt for many years among the Utes. She was there not because she had any desire to return, but because it was required.

She had grown stout with the years, her figure made worse by the shapeless dress of a squaw. Gray streaks coursed raggedly through once dark hair. Moncure recognized the deliberate vacancy in eyes and face, eyes through which shyness and apprehension were barely allowed to show.

Docile but uncooperative, she gave her Indian name willingly enough. It was Fawn at Water. Someone tittered, though plenty of white names became just as incongruous with the passage of years. It was half an hour before she admitted that her white name had been Teresa. What more there might have been, she had forgotten.

Up to now, Miss Samantha DeLoss had watched with an air of shock, replaced by disinterest. A searching glance at the old woman had convinced her that in this unkept creature she could not possibly find the sister she had come seeking. When the name was spoken, she swung about incredulously, fresh shock and disbelief in her eyes.

'It can't be,' she said. 'It's impossible. A DeLoss would never permit herself to be anything but a lady. The name Teresa is not too uncommon.'

Reluctantly, she took part in the questioning, asking about matters pertaining to childhood and family. The quality of the answers remained unchanged. Though compelled to endure this ordeal, it was something in which she took no interest, and for which she felt no concern. Who or what she once had been belonged to the past. Now she was an Indian.

Gradually a few facts were established. Her name really had been Teresa. When other memories faded, that had remained fixed in her mind. A childhood acquaintance had made up a jingle which had impressed her. She recited it as though she were speaking a foreign language, whose words were no longer intelligible.

'Teresa and Samantha, sisters two and twins—

Alike in face, but strange in name and race!'

Samantha DeLoss paled, her voice barely above a whisper.

'There was a boy who was always teasing us, and he made that up! It seemed so silly—strange in name and race! I hated it, but Teresa used to repeat it. Somehow it caught her fancy. But it can't be!'

Apparently it was. The time of Teresa's captivity seemed about right. She had been a small girl, and she retained few memories of the time prior to her life with the Indians. Hesitantly she admitted that she might have had a sister, a white sister, but she looked at Samantha without recognition or particular interest. She was Fawn at Water; she had had a husband, but he was dead; and she had two sons and a daughter. A gleam of pride crept into eyes and voice when she spoke of them.

The horror in Miss Samantha's eyes deepened at the certainty that this half-savage creature must actually be her sister, while a New England conscience prompted her to ask more questions. Again, one drew a response. It concerned a doll with golden hair which both sisters had cherished and had occasionally quarreled over. Its right leg had been broken off in such a quarrel on the day before Teresa had been taken captive.

Her eyes lighted up at the memory, and she looked at her sister with a gleam of

132

remembered hate. Samantha DeLoss brought the doll from the folds of her dress and extended it. Fawn at Water, stared, then snatched it.

In this first ordeal of questioning, the excitement and adventure had gone out of the quest, not alone for Miss Samantha, but for most of the others who had come, seeking lost relatives. It was plain enough that family and pride were forgotten, and would not be restored merely by the magic of restoration to the bosom of a family. To Teresa, family meant a tepee and its occupants, not a centuries-old mansion from which a governor and a senator had gone forth.

If compelled, Fawn at Water would go with this alien woman, but for neither of them would there be any joy in the reunion, any promise or hope in the future. Fawn was an Indian. To be torn a second time from family and friends was at least as frightening as the first experience had been. With the resilience of childhood, that other experience had soon been overcome. Now, for an old woman, far older than her twin, change would be difficult.

The next captive who was brought was a different story. Ben Dodge was eleven years old, and he had been a captive less than a year. He had resisted fiercely all attempts to change him, and he was anxious to go back to the life he had known, to be free of the

Indians. It was not too usual a case, but this time it appeared there was reason for rejoicing.

'I want to see my folks again,' he said, 'my Dad and Mom. How are they?'

Consulting the records which had been supplied him, Colonel Neilson had to tell him. Ben's mother was back at their old home and would be delighted to have him returned. His father, however, had died of wounds suffered when the Indians had attacked.

The boy stood a moment, assimilating the news, and despite his training among the Indians, his lip twitched. Then he turned, shaking a fist at his erstwhile companions.

'So you killed him, did you?' he shrilled. 'Well, as soon as I'm big enough, I'm coming back and kill Indians! Thousands of 'em!'

Sobbing with rage, humiliated also that he should display such a lack of stoical qualities before those he hated, the boy was led away.

★   ★   ★

Oldhouse or Gervais, the name meant little; Hunk had cast aside family pride for immediate and immense profits, since under the circumstances the two were not compatible. The profits had accrued, though somehow money had a way of slipping through his fingers, presenting the ever recurring necessity of securing more.

What counted was that David Dunstan
Moncure knew both his names and the record
which went with both, and Hunk Gervais was
apprehensive. There might be an undeclared
truce at several levels, but it was time to act.
He sought out the Cheyenne chief.

'You have planned a mighty project,' he
reminded Little Wolf, 'which will sweep the
hated enemies of your people forever from the
mountain and the plain, so that your warriors
may again ride tall in the sun. I have been
giving much thought to this, and the thing is
too important to allow anything to interfere or
hinder.'

'It is big,' Little Wolf agreed. 'But nothing
can stop us now. The white men are wary,
but like the pronghorns, they are curious, and
they walk into our trap.'

'That is so,' Gervais agreed. 'They are
indeed wary, highly suspicious. One among
them should be removed at once. The man in
a captain's uniform, called Moncure.'

Little Wolf's eyes grew hooded. 'The plan
is to strike all at once, when the time is right,'
he reminded. 'Anything else would cause
alarm. We await but two things—the guns
which you have promised, and the arrival of
the warriors of the Blackfeet, who are on their
way. Then we will strike.'

'You are undoubtedly the greatest leader
your people has ever known,' Gervais
commented, and the compliment was sincere.

135

Anyone who could persuade the haughty Blackfeet to join in such a league, with rival tribes of so diverse a nature, was indeed formidable.

'As for the guns, you know how and by whose hand they were made to vanish. So it becomes still more important that he be dealt with at once, in one way or another. Perhaps he might be persuaded to lead you to them,' he added. 'But it must be done now!'

That was the wrong note to take. Little Wolf was proud, and resentful of dictation. After all, this man, though an ally, was white, and the day when any white man could dictate was past. Little Wolf did not sense any incongruity in his position. He was not white.

'The man was my brother,' he reminded Gervais. 'He does his duty as he sees it. When all white men die, he will be among the slain. Yet, because of what once was—I cannot strike him in the back.'

'He is white, and you are Indian,' Gervais protested. 'How then can he be your brother?'

'How is the moon brother to the sun, when one is lord of the night, the other of the day? Yet it is so. This man is not my brother, but he was my brother. Because he once was, I owe him an ancient debt.'

From that position he could not be moved. Indians could be as stubborn and crazy as

136

white men. Put the combination together, and you had an unpredictable individual.

Yet action was imperative, action which could not be traced back to Gervais himself. That part would be easy. Once the thing was done, he'd act swiftly, as Indian agent, spiriting the man away, holding him for judgment.

Not all men, red or white, were as complex as Little Wolf or his brother. Gervais' smile broadened. He had just the proper man in mind, one who would be eager to do his bidding. Gervais sought him out.

Coyote Man was a Pawnee. Clad splendidly in the full panoply of a brave, he stalked about, the personification of what a warrior should be. Still under the age of twenty, he was half a head taller than most other men of his tribe, a splendid physical specimen. Only those who knew him well realized the imperfections which prevented him from ever becoming a warrior.

He strutted, to the delight not only of younger boys of his own tribe, but also of other tribes. A fair-sized entourage followed at his heels, despite the reproving glances of their elders. Whenever a good occasion presented itself, Coyote Man grew boastful, repeating some of the secret councils which he had overheard.

'What is this?' he demanded, looking about at the various widespread tribal encampments, and encompassing them with the disdainful sweep of an arm. 'Do I behold braves, mighty warriors gathered for a powwow, to plan battle? Or do I see only a bunch of old women? Where is the glory of the red man, of which so much was said so short a while ago? Where are guns with which to fight? Have we any warriors, or are there no chiefs among us? Must I lead?'

Of the older ones who understood, most shook their head in pity and walked on. Only the younger boys cheered. Coyote Man halted, scowling.

'What is this that I see?' he demanded. 'Is it a Pawnee, who thus approaches the camp of the Pawnees unchallenged? Or is it a white man, who never before would dare such a thing? And shall he dare it now?'

Coyote Man carried a rifle, an ancient weapon of formidable size. Abruptly he lifted it, centering the muzzle on the unknowing back of Moncure. Then the Indian pulled the trigger. *This* would show who was a real warrior, a man with daring. After today, the braves as well as the boys would cheer when Coyote Man appeared.

CHAPTER TWELVE

Moncure swung about, startled, at the blast of the gun. Then he shrugged understandingly and walked on, as other Pawnees, attracted by the commotion, hurried to surround Coyote Man and hustle him away, one meanwhile pointing significantly to his forehead.

Gervais, watching from another vantage point, tugged at a tuft of golden whisker and shook his head. Too late he understood. They permitted the boy to play with a gun, even to charge it with powder, but made sure that he caused no mischief with a ball to the powder.

Never before had any of the chieftains, particularly of the Cheyenne, refused a request when he made one. Not only did he speak as the representative of the Great White Father, the one who had power either to give gifts or to withhold them, but he had supplied them with modern rifles. Naturally he did that at a handsome profit, but nonetheless it filled a need.

To be snubbed in such fashion, whatever reasons Little Wolf might have, was insufferable. Little Wolf must be dealt with.

But how? That was important. It would not do to appear to take offense, to interfere with the plans already under way. But the plans

139

would work out of themselves in a very few days, and if Moncure was dealt with, they would succeed—temporarily at least and well enough for his purpose. The important part was to remain in command—

He nodded, pleased with an idea which until then had been nebulous. There was a way.

It would mean swallowing his pride, acting as though nothing had happened—even appearing to take Little Wolf's judgment above his own. Still, the result should be worth the cost.

Later in the day, Gervais presented himself at the tepee of the chief.

'I have been giving much thought to the matter which we discussed,' he announced gravely. 'At first I doubted the wisdom of your course, but reflection has convinced me that it is the wisest one. We must do nothing to stir the leaves of suspicion until all can be blown loose as in a mighty wind.'

Little Wolf heard him in a silence tinged with expectancy. The agent carried a bundle; therefore he came with a gift, a peace offering. An unbending attitude was the part of wisdom; otherwise Gervais might try to withhold a part of the gift.

'I have something for my friend, the great chief of the nation of Cheyennes,' Gervais went on, and shook out the bundle with a quick motion, holding it outspread, displaying it by two corners. Despite himself, the eyes of Little Wolf flickered, and he put out a hand, then drew it back. The pleasure and desire in his eyes burned like fire.

In some respects, though he would have denied it hotly, he was as white as he had ever been, but in others he had become completely Indian. It took but a glance to see that this blanket was finely woven, scarlet with a strong pattern, thus greatly to be desired. Buffalo robes, which were easy to obtain, were warm and comfortable, but so gaudy a blanket was rare.

'This is a chief's robe,' Gervais added, and the golden cascade of beard concealed a small smile. It had indeed been a chief's, but what Little Wolf did not know would not hurt him—at the moment. 'Wear it proudly.'

Little Wolf accepted the gift with becoming dignity, wrapping it about his shoulders. It was a satisfying moment. Not only had he demonstrated his leadership, over and above that of the white man, but in suing for peace, Gervais had acknowledged it. Little Wolf would indeed walk proudly.

The task of questioning the captives, identifying who they once had been, and seeking to discover whether or not they still possessed any living relatives, went forward endlessly. Even Moncure was somewhat surprised at the number of repatriates. On the surface, at least, the red men were carefully

141

observing the terms of the agreement.

That the majority of these were men, trained warriors and skillful in attack from ambush, did not escape Moncure. Still, everything appeared natural enough.

The work was disheartening, enlivened only occasionally by a flash of warmth or humor. The reunion between two brothers began on a bleak note, the Pawnee brave disdainful of any white, not at all eager to know or acknowledge such a relative. Then he caught sight of his brother's wooden leg, a peg upon which he walked with a roll and a lurch, and the oddity of it took the Indian's fancy. That the limb had originally been lost in the raid in which the Pawnee brother had been carried away did not interest him, but he admired so unusual a limb. Presently they were chatting together, in excellent humor.

For the most part the camps were somnolent, waiting in a sort of lethargy, except when hunters rode out to return with meat. There was an abundance of game on every side, so that was a simple chore. The exception were the Cheyennes. This was their country, and some of them were constantly on the go. Moncure had only to look out to see parties of braves, riding with apparent aimlessness, yet traversing and recrossing the route which he had taken that day with the load of rifles.

Clearly, those guns were vital to their

plans. However much of a mockery these ceremonies might be, they were buying time on both sides.

Karl Hochhalter pursued his own way in the face of the threat. Triumphantly he reported to Moncure, exhibiting a small but carefully wrapped package.

'Now I have the wherewithal to act, should the need arise—as I suspect it will,' he explained. 'I had dispatched a messenger to Starke the same day on which I found the old chief dying in his tepee, urgently requesting that they forward me a good supply of vaccine. I was not at all sure if it could be obtained, so I'll confess that I'm surprised, but here it is. It seems that my fellow practitioner at Starke had been troubled by the same nightmare which haunts us, and had himself ordered a liberal supply. So, praises be, we have it.'

'The forethought which both of you have shown is commendable,' Moncure conceded, 'though the situation is ironic. We may come to pray for just such an epidemic to strike among the tribes, to decimate them, as an alternative to their doing the same to us.'

'True enough,' Hochhalter admitted. 'Perverse are the uses of adversity. But whatever may impend, I must remain true to my calling, which is that of healing.'

'True enough,' Moncure echoed. 'And again we find irony, in that, being a man of peace, you chose a career in the Army.'

'Did not you do the same? To prevent a war is the best way of winning it.'

Moncure laughed, without humor. 'You are not only a healer but a logician,' he observed. 'I wish that I could see some way for putting such philosophy to use.'

'What about confronting that brother of yours with the facts? He, as a white man, is subject to the same rules as are laid down for all the rest. If we had him in our camp, under close observation—'

'It strikes me that he considers himself above the rules which bind lesser men. I've thought of doing that. But to make the demand and try to enforce it could precipitate the attack we're hoping to avoid.'

'I'm afraid you're right,' Hochhalter admitted. 'I grant that for you this is a bitter dose, David—finding your brother again, and in such guise.'

'It's about what I'd expected, though I hadn't guessed that he might be such a famous chief,' Moncure confessed. 'As it is, I've no wish even to try to make a white man of him again. The effort would be foredoomed to failure. But if there were only some way of meeting him on a common ground, of being friendly—'

He walked on as the doctor turned back, strolling at the rim of the military encampment, careful to walk in the open where all might see, not venturing beyond an intangible but definite line. Boldness was essential, but not rashness.

During the week that this business had been under way, he had had no glimpse of the one he most sought, no word concerning her. Some of the Kiowas had put in an appearance, since the gathering was becoming increasingly cosmopolitan. Yet if Stephanie was still alive, still among them, she would probably be held back, not brought there regardless of pact or treaty.

Then, as though his thought had conjured her up, he saw her.

She was walking some distance ahead, near the rim of the Cheyenne camp. A luxuriant hedge of brush screened the rim of the canyon beyond; chokecherry and service berries, the latter taking on a tint of red, were another proof that the summer was on the wane. Whatever Little Wolf might plan, it could not much longer be delayed. This was fighting weather, hunting time, before winter should strike.

That it was Stephanie, Moncure knew at once. She had not seen him, since she was heading the other way, but despite the differences wrought by a score of months, he was sure. Taller than most women, white or red, she had always been a striking figure. Now she was attired as an Indian, but some things were beyond disguise.

Her hair, in which the gold of summer and the red of autumn seemed to mingle, was worn in a braided rope of bronze, falling as far as her waist. The slight saucy swing with which once she had walked was gone, though she still swung along with an easy gait approaching blitheness, as though life still held its quota of pleasant surprises. Desert sun and prairie wind had been unable to modify the fairness of her face.

The one-piece dress of soft white buckskin left her arms bare to the shoulders. Thickly studded with beads, the many colors made a rainbow in the sun. Moncure caught his breath, not only at the beauty revealed, but at certain characteristics of the garment. An Indian woman was possessed of vanity, as suggested by the beads, but was unlike her white sisters in that styles in clothing did not change, and certain patterns were maintained.

Not only was she walking in the camp of the Cheyennes, but this was the outfit of a woman of the Cheyennes, not of the Kiowas. Yet she had been carried away by raiders from the Kiowa.

That she had been traded to the Cheyennes was not particularly surprising. Such a woman would be hard to hide, even in a wilderness, and for many months he had pursued a relentless search. Among a different tribe it would be easier.

Careless of the risk, Moncure started forward. This was one captive who had been kept carefully out of sight, one whom the red men clearly did not intend to return.

'Stephanie!'

She halted, started to turn, but checked that impulse as though in terror, poised like a wild creature on the verge of flight. Then, very slowly, she turned and looked at him, and he knew that she must have heard about him, perhaps watching from a distance. Recognition was in her eyes, while other emotions washed across her face. They ran the gamut from joy to dismay, apprehension and timidity.

She waited, her face drained of color, as he approached. It was clear that any possible pleasure in the encounter was dwarfed by other and less pleasant emotions.

'Stephanie!' he repeated, and halted a few paces away. 'Is it really you?'

She considered the question as gravely as she eyed him, slowly shaking her head. Her emotions had been brought under control.

'No,' she denied, 'it isn't. I'm not Stephanie, David—not any more.'

Here, along with her ready use of his own name, was the contradiction of duality, of white and red in one person. After watching and listening to some of the others in recent days, he found that easy to understand, if not to comprehend. He knew that the inward

147

struggle must be tearing her apart.

Moncure's own emotions seemed frozen, but his tongue refused to credit the evidence of his mind.

'You are Stephanie,' he insisted. 'I've looked everywhere for you—searched and hoped, Stephanie.'

'I know,' she agreed, and a remembered softness, a wistful quality, momentarily warmed her eyes. Then the look faded. 'I'm sorry, but that's all over, David; over and ended. We can never go back.'

Even her accent was different, as though English words no longer fitted properly on her tongue. She was making an effort to make him understand, and he had no trouble doing so, even while one part of him cried out against acceptance, against such a perversion of truth. Yet the bitter accuracy of her ultimatum could not be doubted.

'You have a husband among the Cheyennes, then?' he asked, and despite his certainty as to what the reply would be, the quality of it jolted him.

'A husband, and a son,' she replied, and her face lighted; the tones held a ring of pride.

Somehow, this was no more than he should have expected; actually, he had anticipated that it would be so. It was either that, or slavery, for a captive woman, and the one fate was far worse than the other. He'd seen drudges among the Indians, red women and white alike, though for the whites it was worse.

Stephanie was meeting his gaze proudly, as though daring him either to pity or censure her. Still feeling the need to explain, she tried to do so.

'Things change, David. Life changes. It would have been impossible for me to go back. Besides,' and pride and defiance thrilled in her voice, 'I am a woman of the Cheyenne. I would not go back to the old, even if I could.'

She was saying two things, stating twin facts which complemented each other even while they contradicted themselves. She had made the best of a difficult situation and had come to like it, to take a measure of pride in her new position. Acceptance was not so hard, for one who understood the wide gulf which separated a white woman from the world of which she once had been a part.

A white man might go among the Indians if he chose, becoming a blanket Indian, then return to his old life without particular comment or censure from either white or Indian. Those who chose to do such a thing seldom moved in a stratum of society which found much difference between the two modes of life.

A white boy, taken captive, belonged in a different category. Gradually, insidiously, he became an Indian, hating all things white; it seemed a necessary part of such a life to reject completely the old in taking on the new. In his new life, he found complete acceptance from his fellow tribesmen.

With a white woman the situation was different. Even if she wanted to return, a gulf had arisen which she could no longer cross; a form of ostracism, mingled of scorn and pity, which could never quite be lived down. Aware that it was so, she found it easier to accept the inevitable, to become as Indian as any of the others.

The situation was at once better, yet worse, than Moncure had feared. There was no need to ask how hard and bitter the early days of her captivity must have been. Probably the transition for the Sabine women had been just as difficult, or for similar captives in a thousand episodes of history. The strong who refused to bend were usually broken instead. It showed a certain measure of character for a woman to adapt to the inevitable, to gather up the pieces and build a new life, even to find in it a measure of contentment if not of happiness.

She was looking to the side; and following her glance, Moncure felt a new wave of coldness. No words were needed to explain the situation, as Little Wolf stepped out from the brush and took his stand beside her.

CHAPTER THIRTEEN

The confusion which was attendant upon so large and diverse an encampment, coupled with the details of the repatriation, was both an annoyance and a benefit. Able to hobble on crutches, Old Sam had been forced to move from the bunk of the cabin to a tepee. Never before, since he had worked as a handy man for Hunk Gervais, had he seen anything to approach the numbers of people, the hubbub of crowds. Always a recluse, the old trapper disliked any gathering larger than could be counted on the fingers of his two hands.

On the other hand, with so many people from diverse tribes stirring about, it was possible to come and go almost unnoticed. His broken leg had knit sufficiently so that it was no great problem. So, again making use of the crutches, he edged out from the tepee, then worked his way toward the cabin. Time had been heavy on his hands.

A cautious look around was reassuring. No one was taking any notice of him, and the cabin was empty. Sam ducked inside quickly.

As he had hoped, Gervais still had a flask of whiskey concealed among the pile of buffalo robes. The bottle was new, virtually untouched. Clutching it eagerly, Sam hesitated, since any appreciable lowering of the contents would be noticeable. Then, his craving for liquor overcoming apprehension, he drew out the cork and drank.

A sound at the doorway caused him to swing suddenly, the near-panic making him teeter wildly on one crutch. He regained his balance, his face cleared as he recognized the intruder. Coyote Man, for all his impressiveness of build and bearing, was classed as a half-wit, either teased or idolized by the boys, tolerated by others, and generally harmless.

The Pawnee was staring avidly at the flask which Sam clutched, and there was no mistaking his eagerness. He advanced a step, extending his own hand.

'Give!' he commanded imperiously. Seeing the old man's reluctance, he added impressively, 'Coyote Man heap big chief.'

'Coyote Man heap big fool,' Sam returned contemptuously, but his scowl was apprehensive. It was bad enough to be given so unpleasant a turn, and his injured limb had just given a painful twinge. To be forced to share the liquor would be worse, for then there would be no hiding the fact that the bottle had been tampered with.

Yet if he refused, the would-be brave would be certain to raise a ruckus. He was smart enough to realize that his condition gave him the status of a privileged character, and he was not above taking full advantage of it.

Sam thrust the bottle toward him with a sign of relief. The solution of his own problem was obvious and perfect. Let the fool drink as much as he pleased. All the blame for the thievery would fall upon him, and he'd soon be too drunk to tell a coherent or believable story.

Coyote Man accepted the bottle eagerly, putting the flask to his mouth and choking on the fiery potation, as Old Sam hobbled discreetly away. Finding himself in full possession of the bottle, with no one to interfere, Coyote man sank down on the pile of buffalo skins and made the most of the unexpected windfall.

When he emerged from the cabin some quarter of an hour later, the empty bottle had been discarded and his eyes had taken on a glassy stare, but no one paid much attention to him as he made his way out from the camp, heading aimlessly across the plain. Thunder muttered in the distance, and a few drops of rain were beginning to spatter, but he paid no heed to the storm, walking on and on. This, the first rain since the rain which had fallen on that day when Moncure had driven the wagon with its load of supposed garden tools, was welcome not only to the parched earth but to Coyote Man, whose mouth and throat seemed on fire.

The rain died away, then came on with renewed violence, long sweeping sheets blanketing the landscape like fog. It was pleasantly cooling, and the exercise was beneficial, so that he was feeling exhilarated, very well satisfied with himself and the world in general. It was not often that so pleasant a gift came his way.

Something brought him up short, jarring him painfully. Coyote Man gazed around owlishly, puzzled and somewhat annoyed. Gradually he understood what had happened, still annoyed rather than alarmed. He had blundered against a pole, out there in the open where no trees were supposed to be; this was one of several, erected to hold platforms on which dead warriors reached closer to the sun.

The graves overhead were all about; the confusion was rendered worse by the driving rain and beating wind, in which loose streamers of blankets or buffalo skin flapped eerily.

Normally, Coyote Man would have been badly frightened. He was by no means so stupid as not to understand the sacredness of this spot of ground onto which he had blundered, and even if the spirits of the departed ones did not hover unpleasantly about, still the anger of the Cheyennes who were still alive could be a terrible thing.

In his present state of mind he had no fear

of anything, living or dead. His mood was of annoyance, first that such a pole should get in his way, secondly that these insults to the sky should have been placed by the hated Cheyennes. His mood of resentment had been simmering for the past several days, and now it was ready to boil. Even the warriors of the Pawnee fawned upon the Cheyenne chief, Little Wolf, a situation which Coyote Man considered both humiliating and disgraceful.

There was talk of war, such as had rung in the councils these many moons, and that he could understand; still there was no war, and that he could not comprehend. It was increasingly clear that the Pawnees needed a leader, a daring warrior such as himself. If only he had a gun—a real one, which would shoot—

Staring upward, his mouth gaped in amazement. Truly, his medicine must be strong, for this was like an answer to prayer. Not far overhead, partly visible where the worrying wind had torn away the wrappings, a rifle barrel thrust out. Coyote Man took a deep breath and began to climb.

★　　★　　★

The Cheyenne chief eyed Moncure haughtily, glancing possessively at the squaw with auburn tresses. Understanding, Moncure drew a slow breath in which many emotions

155

were mingled. Here was supreme irony. This woman had first attracted him, and it was not strange that his brother had found her desirable when beholding her under other circumstances.

'My squaw,' Little Wolf pronounced proudly. That he had overheard enough of the conversation to understand the situation was evident. He glared defiantly. 'Little Wolf keep!'

Stephanie looked from one to the other, her eyes troubled, apprehensive. Moncure doubted if she had known that he was anywhere in that part of the country until he had called to her a short while before.

In one way, time was like a running brook. Its waters, trickling gently along a mountain meadow, questing and hesitant, bore only a superficial resemblance to the headlong swirl of a river pouring to the sea. Yet one thing was forever unchanged. Once a man was embarked upon that journey, there could never be any turning back.

'You are his—' Moncure could not bring himself to say either wife or squaw. Stephanie nodded.

'That is so, David,' she agreed. 'For more than a year now. I never expected to see you again,' she added pleadingly. 'Even if I had—' She allowed the words to trail off, but he sensed all the hopelessness which they implied.

Little Wolf scowled. He had a wider knowledge of many things than most men of his adopted race, but he had Probably not realized, until now, that there could ever have been anything between this woman and his white brother. She did not yet fully appreciate the situation. Little Wolf felt both humiliated and angry, proud and fiercely possessive at the same time.

Guiltily, Moncure realized that he was both relieved and pleased by this unexpected turn of events. They had loved each other, he and Stephanie, but that had belonged, quite literally, to another life. Time had done more than thrust them apart, erecting a barrier never to be crossed.

By whatever name she was called, she was Little Wolf's woman, and his own bitter awareness, never quite acknowledged, that Stephanie was lost to him had made a difference to Moncure. Into that troubled void had come Serena, her own heart sore from a personal loss.

He had a dull conviction that in such a situation there was nothing to be said. Still, words had to be spoken. Moncure took refuge in the obvious.

'I don't blame you for wanting to keep her, Little Wolf,' he acknowledged. 'But have you forgotten the purpose of this gathering, which is to return all white captives to their own people?' He prodded him sharply. 'You are a chief of the Cheyennes. Is this the manner in which you honor an agreement?'

It was then that the stubborn streak which was a trait of the Moncures became apparent in his brother. Little Wolf's jaw jutted.

'She is my wife,' he said, this time using the white term rather that the Indian, 'the mother of my son. She does not want to go back. Nor would I ever give her up!'

Stephanie had been standing with downcast eyes, her face flushing and paling by turns, her hands twisting together. Aside from Moncure, there was no one left among her former people, no parents, brothers or sisters. Now she stole a glance at Little Wolf, and pride, along with something akin to adoration, was in her eyes. Probably never before had Little Wolf expressed his feelings for her, certainly not in such positive terms.

'You could return together, remain together,' Moncure pointed out. 'You, too, Little Wolf, are a white captive. Have you forgotten?'

Pride and hatred blended in the fiery reply. 'Little Wolf Indian! All Indian! The war chief of the Cheyennes would never become a white man!'

'There are strong men, and honorable, among the red men, and also among the white,' Moncure returned. 'Your mother, Little Wolf—our mother—loved her white sons, and loved them equally. As for me, I have lost a brother whom I also loved.'

A startled light glowed in Stephanie's eyes as she finally understood, looking from one to the other. There was compassion in her gaze, also a hidden dismay at what was implied.

That form of appeal caught the chief off guard. For an instant he was at a loss.

'Little Wolf has no brother—no white brother,' he went on fiercely, almost contemptuously.

'If I owed you any debt as a brother, I have paid it. Not many suns ago, my warriors were angry with me; they strained like hounds at the leash, desiring to kill you, along with those who had been in the stagecoach. They were bitterly disappointed when I refused to allow them to seize even the scalps of those already dead.'

He paused, and a darker surge of color ran over his cheeks, as though he were ashamed of himself for such a womanish display of emotion, a softness not to be expected in a Cheyenne. Moncure stared in amazement, finally understanding the true reason the attack had been called off in the moment of victory instead of being pressed.

'Once we were small boys together,' Little Wolf added. 'Because of that—I held them back.'

That his act had troubled and still plagued him was apparent. It was due to a softness incompatible with an Indian, to a taint of white blood which he had not quite been able to eradicate. Moncure felt a surge of gratitude and admiration, even as he recognized the increased danger which sprang from the act, not only to himself, but to every white in the country. For a man with hatred of all whites in his heart, Little Wolf had acted generously. He had paid any debt which might exist between them.

Now suddenly there was a fresh reason for hatred, the knowledge that this woman, his woman, had once loved this white man, who was also his brother. The thought must rankle. Rage smoldered in his eyes, mixed with reluctant admiration. He was a war chief of the Cheyennes, and that was a proud and desirable state; but this brother, though white, was also a great leader, with a reputation known on both sides of the Border.

'I did not know or understand how it happened,' Moncure admitted. 'I had wondered about it. You acted generously.'

Little Wolf grunted absently. He, too, was at a loss to explain especially with this woman between them. Though he would never have admitted it, he was somewhat in awe of her and always had been, was secretly amazed at his good fortune in having won her for his own. Life, quite suddenly, was not so simple as it had seemed.

'Much has happened which is surprising,'

Moncure added. 'To all of us, I think.' He inclined his head. 'May I wish you happiness—both of you?'

Little Wolf glared uncertainly. There was a sudden rush of tears to Stephanie's eyes which she sought to control, becoming aware that her man was guilty of no such softness. Once this moment was past, Moncure realized, these revelations would make no difference in the Cheyenne's plan to destroy all whites. He had yielded once to sentiment, and if there had been any bond, any debt remaining from boyhood, he accounted it paid.

A moment longer they stared from one to the other. Then Little Wolf gestured and stalked away. Stephanie looked back once, then followed obediently a couple of steps behind.

CHAPTER FOURTEEN

Coyote Man came swaggering, with the air of a conqueror. His somewhat confused mind found it easy to believe that he had already performed an outstanding feat, both of discovery and valor. The potent effects of the whiskey had not entirely worn away.

Over either shoulder was a rifle, a burden which several times had managed almost to

161

trip him, since slung to the barrels of the guns was assorted booty—gifts to the dead, some of which had been buried with the dead, others piled at a respectful distance from the graves in the sky. These were prizes taken in war or painfully purchased. It had seemed right and proper to Coyote Man that he should take of what was so bountifully at hand.

The rifles were the real prize, and about them there was no confusion in his mind. Guns were the tools of war, instruments in the winning of wars. Now he knew the secret of the lost rifles, which the stupid Cheyennes, for all their desperate searching, had been unable to discover.

He came to the edge of the camps, where they confronted each other after the manner of distrustful adversaries, the white men on one hand and the Cheyennes not far away. It was some distance on to the village of the Pawnees, but in his exalted mood Coyote Man was equally contemptuous of white and Cheyenne.

Halting, he brandished a rifle in a defiant gesture, allowing some of his trophies to spill as he did so. Sight of some of the men of his own tribe, lounging not far off, increased his confidence.

'The Cheyennes are a nation of old women,' he announced. 'Such wisdom as they possess is in the graves of their dead! For many days they have hunted wildly to find guns, but it required a warrior of the Pawnees to discover the rifles, clutched in the hands of the dead!'

Moncure had noticed Coyote Man as he approached the camp, curiously laden. He was close enough now to hear the words, at which he felt a sudden chill. It was as though a wintry wind had risen abruptly out of the heart of summer, scattering disaster and death in its wake. His thoughts, somber as they had been for the last hour or so, were wrenched away from his own troubles.

A momentary hush followed Coyote Man's pronouncement, a silence of shock and disbelief. Additional men of the Cheyenne appeared, almost like those wraiths of which the Pawnee spoke so disrespectfully, conjured into life. Then a growl of outrage commenced, swelling as the Cheyennes sensed what an impiety had been committed—the desecration of sacred places by the hand of an enemy.

Only two things held them back from swift action, from retaliation upon this rash lout. The one was astonishment at what he had proclaimed, and which the flourished rifle seemed to prove: that he had indeed found the missing guns. Even in the midst of shock and anger, they were eager to learn more. The other was the knowledge that this man was one of the simple ones, not quite responsible for what he might say or do.

Even so, such desecration had to be avenged, swiftly, terribly. If it was impossible fully to punish a man with a twisted mind, still there were his people, who automatically shared his guilt.

Moncure listened with mixed emotions. Here was dynamite, with the fuse already burning, dangerously close to the explosive point. He was both elated and dismayed.

In one sense, this could prove an answer to the Army's problem. For if civil strife erupted between Cheyenne and Pawnee, the struggle would inevitably spread to engulf the other tribes. Never had the stage been set for so deadly or devastating a struggle, one so unreasoning in its fury.

One problem would be automatically solved. All thought of unity among the red men, of a common war against the whites, would vanish, never to be revived. The tribes would be decimated, weakened past recovery, by the slaughter that would follow.

In that process, a myriad of lesser problems would be taken care of. Death would be a common leveler.

It would be too common, too impartial, and completely color blind. The Army would have no choice but to intervene to try to keep the peace. Even if it chose to remain aloof, it would not be allowed to do so. By now the knowledge was fairly common, at least among

164

the Cheyennes, that it was Moncure who had diverted those guns from their grasp. Such awareness had whetted their eagerness for the coming strike, and in their minds, the Army shared responsibility for all which had happened, or might yet occur.

Nor would Hunk Gervais use his influence to try and hold back his charges. Total massacre was one way of wiping a stained record from the book.

Most of all, there was Little Wolf, thirsty for war, his mind filled now with thoughts more confused than ever yet doubly vengeful. Here was the brink of holocaust.

The war chief chose that moment to come striding into the open, an impressive, blanket-wrapped figure. The rising chant of anger hesitated, then fell to a murmur at sight of him.

Motivation with an Indian was not the same as with a white man, and in this hour Little Wolf was fiercely, proudly Indian. It was expressed and epitomized in the gaudy blanket, such as only a chief might possess. And his action would be doubly impressive when he cast it aside, the gesture a call to war.

In that instant the blanket seemed grimly appropriate. It was the one in which Old Bear had died.

Little Wolf scowled impartially upon Coyote Man and upon his own braves, crouching like wolves in whose nostrils the scent of blood came ever more rankly. Like Moncure, Little Wolf had been close enough to hear the Pawnee's boasting, and with understanding came both dismay and wild fury. Such an insult to the dead of his people, even by a half-wit, could not be overlooked.

On the other hand, the mystery of the missing rifles was solved, and one part of his mind was filled with a grudging admiration for the ingeniousness of the cache. Moncure had chosen the one possible place where no one would think to look, and, desecration or not, the coveted guns were now to be had for the taking.

That, in this moment, was only a small part of the whole. Until today, his master plan had been all-encompassing, completely simple. All at once, nothing was easy. Personally, there were the revelations about his own squaw, his own brother. And in this, the taking of vengeance against the Pawnees, would lie the ruin of all his plans for uniting the tribes in a larger war against the common enemy.

The insult had been offered to the Cheyennes, and as the chief of the Cheyennes he could neither condone nor overlook it. He trembled with eagerness for vengeance, but taking it would be self-defeating. Here were more than Cheyenne and Pawnee. A bloody slaughter would ensue, and when it was over, he would have given the hated white men an unearned victory. Even if every white in the encampment died, all hope of making war against the larger hordes of settlers would die in that same hour.

Moncure thought that he understood the hesitation behind Little Wolf's scowl. He took quick advantage of the pause, rapping out a question.

'Where did you get that blanket?'

Little Wolf stared, startled by the unexpectedness of the query. He had been prepared for almost anything but that, and his bewilderment showed on his face. What did a blanket matter, even the blanket of a chief, in such a moment?

Moncure quickly followed the question with another.

'Did you steal it from the tepee of Old Bear—to bring upon yourself and your people the death from which he sought to save you? I cannot believe that you, my brother, would do such a thing.'

'Old Bear?' Little Wolf repeated, confused. 'Steal? You talk of death? I do not understand.'

Out of the corner of his eye, Moncure saw that Hochhalter was hurrying to reach them. Apparently he too had seen and recognized the blanket, even from a distance. A diversion had been created, and as the others watched uncertainly, Moncure pursued it.

'If you did not steal it from a dying man, where did you get that blanket? Who gave it to you—so that you and your people would catch the disease from its folds and die from plague?'

Rarely did an Indian's face lose color, at least to a noticeable degree, but for all the bitter washing out of white blood, Little Wolf's skin could show the hue of paleness. 'Plague?' he repeated.

'Plague—smallpox,' Moncure amplified. 'Old Bear was a chief, yet when he became old and sick, he thought first of his people, and was willing to sacrifice himself that they might live. For that reason he told no one of his intention, but stole away to die alone. When the sickness began to take hold upon him, he guessed what it was. Dr. Hochhalter found him, but by then it was too late to help.

'The blanket which you wear is the blanket in which Old Bear was dying, and death is in it!'

'Indeed so,' Hochhalter amplified breathlessly, from beside Moncure. 'I returned again to see how the old chief fared. He was dead, so I buried him and burned the wigwam, to keep the plague from spreading, so that he should not have died in vain. Only his blanket had been taken. Now it is about your shoulders!'

Others were gathering, attracted by the commotion, the electric sense of disaster.

There were warriors from several of the tribes, with the Cheyennes predominating; also white families, who had come there seeking the lost. Soldiers stood at the alert, as did some of the women. Marcia Neilson came, with Serena at her side.

Moncure gave no outward sign of having noticed. Actually it made no particular difference. Colonel Neilson was listening with the rest, Sergeant Hauswitz and Lieutenant Slighbull Turner flanking him on either side.

Little Wolf looked from one to the other, his mouth drawing tight at the corners. His gaze came back to the blanket which he had donned so proudly. For once his mind had lost its ability to march with cold precision toward a goal, was jumbled suddenly by a hundred nameless terrors. He spoke reluctantly.

'These things I did not know. Old Bear was my friend. I do not doubt what you say, that the blanket was his, though I had never seen it.' Rage flared suddenly in his eyes and voice. 'You white men are all alike—pretending friendship, then acting treacherously! It was given to me by Gervais!'

Hochhalter nodded briskly, overlooking the innuendo.

'That's as I suspected,' he agreed. 'It was clear in our minds that Little Wolf would never take the robe from a dead man. I feared something like this, for we agree that Gervais is a scoundrel. I can save you and your people, Chief. If you will put yourself in our hands, obey orders, we will manage despite the plotting.'

Little Wolf stared, not entirely understanding, torn between hate and fear, hope and despair. The rage dimmed, leaving a sheen of dullness in his eyes.

'Would I be such a fool as to trust any white man?' he argued, but the question was defensive rather than truculent.

'That you and your people hate and distrust white men we do not question,' Moncure returned soberly. 'There has been much bad faith by many white people—but there has been just as much bad faith on the part of some red men. My father was killed by the Cheyennes. He was your father also, Little Wolf.

'But that belongs to the past. I know what you planned, and it was a great vision, to strike and wipe out all whites from the land of the red men. But what you might have done is no longer possible, because of what has just happened. Should you kill us, then the plague would kill you and those who followed you.'

He paused, allowing Little Wolf a chance to think about that, and its inevitability. An Indian might harbor many doubts, accepting the truth fatalistically, but also striking out in blind rage and despair, regardless of consequences. He based his hope on the fact that Little Wolf, for all his protestations that he was wholly Indian, still thought much as a white man.

'We are brothers, and you saved my life,' Moncure went on. 'I would do as much in turn. Dr. Hochhalter can save you and your people from the plague. Once let it get a start, and it will sweep through all the tribes. I am a soldier, and you have threatened us. You may wonder that we do not allow death to slay as it will. Never again, after that, would white men need to fear the Indian.

'That we could have done, by saying nothing, allowing the plague in the blanket to fasten upon you. But our purpose here is to protect everyone, both white and Indian. Also, there is your wife and your son. Would you have them die when they might live?'

Everyone had fallen silent. Many did not understand the words, but the underlying peril, the sense of drama, was plain. Moncure added quietly:

'Never before, it is said, and I believe it, has there been such a chief among the Cheyennes, great in war, wise in peace. What you command, your people and these others will do. Explain to them the threat of the plague, and tell them that Dr. Hochhalter can save them. They must allow him to make a scratch on the arm of each, to let out the devil already within them. As soon as that has been done, each tribe must return to its own territory. If far apart, there is less danger for all.'

Doubt and hesitation still struggled in Little Wolf's eyes. He understood the principle of vaccination, but he was being asked to play a role contrary to all his experience, all his dreams. The logic of the situation was undeniable, pulling him both ways. Once started, he knew how terribly the plague could sweep. It would decimate the tribes like fire in prairie grass.

If war came now, it would leave them weakened, a ready prey to the greater enemy which the red men were helpless to combat. Their medicine men would be helpless.

Stephanie had listened. Now she moved to stand beside Little Wolf.

'I have been proud of you,' she said softly. 'Do this great thing, and we will share many a harvest moon.'

Little Wolf shrank away from her, knowing the contamination which lurked in the blanket; then he shrugged resignedly. For both of them, as for his people, it was already too late. The only hope lay in yielding, in accepting a white brother's offer.

For himself he did not much care, for his dream was suddenly ended. It was different with Stephanie. He suspected that in many ways he might still be white, for this woman had become more than a casual companion. She meant as much to him as any woman could to any man.

His gaze shifted to Coyote Man, but the rage was all drained out of him. Coyote Man was a foolish one, able to mouth big words, with only a dim understanding of what he said.

'The agent must die,' Little Wolf pronounced flatly. 'He is enemy to his own people and to us alike, dealing treacherously. If you mean what you say—'

'We agree that he must die,' Moncure conceded. A sentence of death, pronounced upon Oldhouse half a decade before, was still in effect. 'Now explain this thing to your people, and to all the people. There is no reason for anyone to be afraid. They must submit to the scratch of a needle, but it is good medicine, and not painful. Dr. Hochhalter is anxious to save lives, and he knows how.'

It did not occur to Little Wolf to look to Colonel Neilson for confirmation of the agreement. His brother had spoken, and that was enough. However fantastic the turn in a strange situation, somehow it seemed reasonable. Then a new and disturbing thought occurred to Little Wolf.

'There can be peace now between the red men and the white,' he admitted. 'But on one point I will not yield. I am an Indian, and this woman is my wife. I cannot return to live among the whites. That is not for me. Nor

173

will I give her up, though we both die!'

Moncure turned to where Myles Neilson had come to stand beside him.

'So far as this conference is concerned,' the colonel returned, 'the threat of plague overshadows all else. You and your wife, Little Wolf, will be needed to lead your people.'

Gratitude showed for an instant in the chief's eyes. Hochhalter took charge.

'Throw your blanket on the fire, Little Wolf. Then set the others an example, as I scratch your arm first of all.'

Little Wolf obeyed. He turned and spoke to the warriors of the Cheyenne, explaining, beating down incipient rebellion when it threatened. They had listened, bewildered, not really understanding, but held under the spell of their leader. His hold over them was manifested anew. Then he spoke to some of the other chiefs. He had great difficulty to persuade them to submit to the white doctor's medicine. To many, that was almost as fearsome as the plague.

His own example was a powerful persuader, and when Miss Samantha DeLoss stepped forward and bared her own arm, then quietly took charge to assist the doctor, the gesture was not lost on them. What a woman could do a warrior ought not to shrink from.

Coyote Man was led away, protesting the peaceful turn of events, reluctantly forced to accept. The effects of the liquor had worn off, leaving him somnolent.

Even the desecration of the graves drew few protests as Little Wolf spoke sharply. The spirits of the departed ones had sent them a sign, and if a foolish one had been the instrument for revealing it, they should accord him honor rather than anger.

Though vigilant, the troops moved with quiet circumspection, well aware of the explosive quality of the huge gathering. That the encampment would be broken up peacefully, each tribe returning to its own country, was a better development than most had dared hope for.

A search for Hunk Gervais was instituted as soon as the general situation was under control. It took some time, and Moncure, like Little Wolf, suspected that the agent had fled while he could. Then they found him, stretched on a pile of buffalo skins, in the tepee which he had been occupying during the encampment.

A look at the man was enough to reveal his condition and his own awareness of his plight. That he was lacking neither in courage nor a sense of humor, Moncure had known. In this crisis, these qualities did not fail the agent.

'It was too late to run.' He shrugged, looking up at the two brothers who stared down at him. A wry smile twisted his mouth beneath the golden beard. 'You've been

175

wanting me dead a long while, Moncure, and your wish will soon be granted. Yours as well, Little Wolf. To think that I made such a mistake!'

'I gave you the blanket, Little Wolf, to get revenge on you, never guessing that handling it might affect me. The way it has worked out, the medico is likely to save you, but for me it is too late. I, praises be, am long past his powers. I had figured for most of my days that I had had the disease as a boy, and so was immune. Now I suppose that it must have been the natural cussedness cropping out of me, for this time it has me, or I have it. Either way, it will save you hanging me, Moncure, a small favor for which I am properly grateful!'

CHAPTER FIFTEEN

It had been a tense twenty-four hours, piled on top of a span of days in which Moncure had taken little pleasure, though in retrospect they might be found to contain certain highlights. Some moments he would not have missed, even if it meant repeating hazard and heartbreak to live over again.

In those days, Serena Sullivan had come into his life, and somehow the emptiness caused by Stephanie's departure was neither

176

so great nor so devastating as it had threatened to be. The heartache had long since run its course.

However hard that two-year period had been for him, the ordeal for her must have been worse. Yet she had found Little Wolf, who in turn had made discoveries which left him both bewildered and pleased. The situation was not what either Stephanie or himself would have chosen, but now she preferred it, and that was a door which would have to remain closed.

Karl Hochhalter had done his best. His forethought, coupled with the unselfishness of the regimental physician at Starke in sending along the requested vaccine, gave them a fighting chance. The only trouble, as Hochhalter wryly explained to Moncure, was that he could inoculate not more than a quarter of the total number of tribesmen.

'A few hundred in all, including such of our own people as have not been treated previously,' he shrugged. 'This is a gathering such as no one had expected. Moreover, we find their numbers on the increase, with a lot of women and children coming in, after keeping well out of sight while trouble threatened. It comes down to a question of addition or subtraction—and not a simple exercise in arithmetic!'

'And your solution?'

Hochhalter grinned tightly.

'Between you and me and the devil, David, I will scratch the arms of all, but some I will give only a dose of water. They'll not know the difference now, and pray God they never may. By dispersing, and after the measures we've already adopted there is a better than even chance that we have stopped it short of an epidemic. If that fails—well, we'll have done our best.'

He was doing his best, working through the night and into the next day, his face graying with fatigue, but pausing only to gulp black coffee or snatch a hasty bite of food as fresh fuel stoked the big fire which gave light to work by.

As both he and Moncure had anticipated, many did not wait to receive the white man's medicine, fearing it almost as much as the plague. They decamped silently during the hours of darkness, so that by dawn of the next day the task was lessened. Enough had been done to cut the hazard.

That morning, too, as though aware that he had nothing more for which to linger, Hunk Gervais died and was swiftly buried. By noon, the camps were breaking up.

If some of the captives vanished with their erstwhile captors, it was no longer a matter for complaint on the part of most who had come so hopefully seeking them. Teresa DeLoss, who would never be a DeLoss again, had been among the number to prefer the only home they knew, the family of which they were a part.

Miss Samantha watched her depart, trudging stolidly among the other squaws while the warriors rode. She shook her head ruefully.

'I'm a wiser woman,' she confessed, 'though sadly disillusioned. But it's better so. She would never be happy back home—not in our old home. All that she knows or cares about is bound up in *her* home—and I've no doubt it would be as hard for me as for her. Speaking selfishly, she would be a burden for both of us, one which neither of us would know what to do with. So dies a dream.'

Yet Miss Samantha might not be returning as she had planned. She had given expert assistance to Karl Hochhalter through the long hours of the night, stony-faced where more emotional women had turned pale at the sight of scratched arms and uneasy patients. Hochhalter had watched with increasing approval, then had given vent to a rare outburst of commendation.

'Miss DeLoss, you should have been a doctor yourself—or at least a doctor's wife!' he blurted, then colored to the roots of his whiskers, realizing how his tongue betrayed him. 'I did not mean—so to speak to a lady of your attainments—was presumptuous—'

'Was it, Karl?' she asked. As Moncure had pointed out, she was still a young and

179

beautiful woman, particularly in that moment. 'What is presumptuous from a man of your attainments, giving his life in such service, under such difficult conditions?'

She added softly. 'I came out to this country seeking for something. Exactly what it was I did not know. Perhaps I have found it—not what I expected, but more to be desired.'

Little Wolf, grave but diffident, came to say goodbye. Stephanie, a new light in her eyes, accompanied him, and this time she walked at his side. Seeing them, Serena came to stand with Moncure.

'In some things I have been mistaken,' Little Wolf confessed. 'I am an Indian—but not entirely so, as I believed. I am pleased and proud to have found my white brother again.'

Moncure gripped the extended hand, feeling some of the old bitterness washed from him.

'I, too, am pleased and proud,' he admitted. 'This is good.'

'Is it any wonder that I loved both of you?' Stephanie asked. She turned swiftly to Serena. 'You will make him happy. We each have found us a man!'

Serena colored faintly, but her eyes were steady. Impulsively, she took Stephanie in her arms and kissed her.

'So must I ever be grateful to you,' she

180

said, and was startled at the impish grin on Little Wolf's face, his unexpected rejoinder. 'Do I, then, receive no credit?' he asked.

Photoset, printed and bound in Great Britain by REDWOOD BURN LIMITED, Trowbridge, Wiltshire